37 Days: Holding on 2 Broken Promises

37 Days, Volume 2

Marissanem

Published by Marissanem, 2024.

Chapter 1

POV X

Pain.

Pain is coursing through my body, mind, and soul.

I can deal with the physical pain, but what I can't seem to get a grip over is the fresh feeling of pain in my heart.

Personally, I've never been heartbroken before. I am always the one breaking someone else's heart, never been on the receiving end.

I broke my baby's heart which completely destroyed mine in the process.

My mind is going a mile a minute as Julian walks me to his room. He's not stupid, he knows bringing me to the penthouse would be a fast trigger.

Trigger.

Millie, with my gun in her hands, pointed at me.

The hate in her beautiful, once so innocent face, carried so much disgust for me that she pointed the most lethal weapon at me, being the target.

I did that, I caused her all that hate she felt. She was so desperate to be anywhere than near me that she felt the need to point a gun at me as a threat.

I know in my heart it was nothing more than a scare tactic, she never turned the safety off and this girl, my girl, knows guns.

"C'mon man, come inside," Julian suggests as he holds his door open for me.

My feet bring me to his gray polyester, too stiff couch. I lean forward, putting my head in my hands.

I swear to god I will die of heartbreak if she's at that prick Chase's house again, but I know Millie, that would be too obvious of a find, I know she can't be there.

"I need to find her," I say desperately.

"We'll find her X, she just needs time," Julian sympathizes.

"No! I need to find her right fucking now!" I spit out.

"My man, she pointed a fucking gun in your face, I don't think she wants to be found right now." He says so matter of fact.

I slam my fists on the wooden coffee table causing a vibration, "I said no!" I yell out half in frustration, half in pain, causing the glass of Millie's iPhone to plunge deeper into my skin.

"Get Stephanie," I say between clenched teeth.

"No, I'm not getting her anymore involved X." Julian quietly but sternly tells me.

"Get her now Julian or so help me god," I threaten.

"X..." he trails off.

"NOW!" I scream out losing my shit.

"Dude, chill, alright I'll go get her, but pull your shit together in front of her, you will not speak to her the way you're speaking to me," Julian demands.

I hate them right now, I hate that they're doing so well, and although they're not rubbing it in my face in any way, it sure fucking feels like it when the other half of me is gone.

Julian leaves to get Stephanie a minute later and it's the first time I'm alone in days, it's the first time I'm alone since my heart feels as though it has become immobile and accelerated all at the same time.

I sit with my hands and head in their previous position and pathetically let warm salty tears run down my face and onto Julian's hardwood floors that I inflicted on myself.

I sit and think about the excruciating pain I caused to the woman I love. She's hurting right now because of me and I can't even protect her or save her from the damage I've done.

Julian disrupts my thoughts by barging through the door, "Dude, X, she's not there. Mia said she left about a half hour ago with her car."

No, the fuck she didn't.

Chapter 2

POV Julian

They've lost it.

These two have completely and utterly lost their minds loving each other.

I'm on my way to the second floor to drag my poor lady into this mess to keep X from going even further off the deep end. He's out of his actual mind right now and I need to be the mediator for them and for this house before it all comes crumbling down because of X's emotions.

I don't know what he expects to come from this. His and Millie's relationship is toxic to one another, because of him. I feel for Millie right now, I want her to sort out her feelings and get the space that not only she needs but also deserves, but X will not let that happen. He always has to be in control of every situation, it's been that way his whole life which makes him a good leader but an awful person at times. He's not in control of this situation, to be honest, he's completely out of control and he knows that. I understand that he fears if enough time passes that losing her would be solidified but at the same time if he doesn't leave her alone for at least a little while, that solidification would become the same result.

In my mind, I think their relationship is fucked. I don't know all the details of what happened when I left but I can just imagine what went down.

My question though is, how did Millie know where X was? In time, I'll find out.

I reach suite number 203 and bring my knuckles to the door knocking lightly.

No answer.

I knock again but with a little more force this time around.

I wait a few seconds before bringing my knuckles into contact again but the handle of the door begins to move.

It's Mia who stands in the doorway.

I scratch the back of my head, "Hey Mia, can you get Steph for me?" I ask to a sleepy, hooded-eyed Mia.

She scrunches her face, bringing her eyebrows towards each other, "Uh, she's not here." She says with a yawn.

"What do you mean she's not here? Where is she?" I ask concerned.

"I have no idea, she rushed in here not too long ago asking for my car keys but she was in a hurry so she didn't tell me anything." She explains.

"Fuck.." I say tensely, dragging my hands down my face.

"Is everything okay? What is going on..?" Mia asks anxiously.

"Yeah, yeah," I say quietly.

I leave a confused Mia in her doorway and make my way back to my place, walking nervously step after apprehensive step.

X is going to flip his shit.

I reach my door and take a deep breath, exhaling louder than I intended.

What a fucked day it's been already, and now more to come.

I walk in and X is sitting in the same spot, in the same depressed position.

I've never in my 30 years of existence seen X cry. It's actually an uncomfortable sight but I get it, if I just lost Steph in an instant I'd be crying like a fucking baby right now too.

I deliver the bad news to X and a switch visibly goes off in his head.

"She lied to me?! Stephanie fucking lied to my face?!" He roars out.

Shit....

"We don't know that X," I offer out.

He scoffs at me.

"Maybe she's out looking for her, don't make assumptions, especially about my lady, you're the one that fucked up here," I say without remorse.

"I know, okay! I fucking know!" X growls through clenched teeth, I wouldn't be surprised if he grinded his teeth off at this point.

"Call ray right fucking now to find them." He demands.

"Dude, it's like 6 in the morning…" I start to say but get cut off by my agitated friend.

"Call him now, I won't ask again." He threatens.

"Fine," I say with my hands up in surrender.

"When I get this information though X, don't go fucking up, I don't trust you right now." I say as sternly as I can and start to walk away into my in-home office, but not before I hear him say in a calmer tone,

"That makes two of us."

Chapter 3

POV X

My mind is frantic, Julian has been in his office for two minutes and it feels like it's been an eternity.

I'm pacing around the living room, the adrenaline is starting to subside and the pain from the glass in my hand that is surrounded by dried blood is starting to take its effect on me. I try to take shards out to occupy my mind until Julian comes back.

I get out the larger pieces of glass the best I can but there are still smaller, deeper ones claiming my hand as their home.

Julian walks out of his office, painfully slow.

I rush over to him unable to bear another second of not knowing where the girl I love is.

"What did you find out?" I ask eagerly.

"Well..X, there's not much to tell, he'll try to locate Steph through her phone but even if we track Steph, that doesn't necessarily mean she's with Millie. He'll call us with any updates and he can't exactly track Millie's phone given it's partially in your hand..." Julian explains while pointing his index finger at my bloodied hand.

I nod my head feeling disappointed by the lack of information.

Back to square one.

"I'll call Evelyn to get that hand cleaned up, Ang you go get a fucking shirt on," Julian says going back into his office.

I walk into Julian's room pulling a black t-shirt out of the closet and dragging my head through while I wait for Evelyn.

Evelyn is Slim's sister, she's our medic. She doesn't live in the house, she has a job at a hospital and does side work for us when we need it so it doesn't raise any red flags.

I look closer at my fucked up hand and feel the pain grow stronger.

I turn on the notifications for the outdoor camera just in case Steph comes back soon, I need to drill her for questions.

...

It's been 20 minutes since Julian called Evelyn and she's just arrived with a bag of medical supplies in hand.

She gestures for me to sit at the small kitchen table which carries the most light. She pulls out tweezers, rubbing alcohol, a needle, a magnifying glass, and a bandage wrap.

"Wash the blood off your hands, Xavier," Evelyn says without even looking at me.

I do as I'm told, carefully drying my hands with a towel, and sit back down.

She goes to work trying to get the shards out as carefully as possible and it's hurting like a motherfucker but I'd never say that out loud.

She places tiny pieces of glass onto a paper towel, I feel like I'll be here all day getting this out.

My phone dings in the pocket of my jeans. I pull it out with my free hand, camera notification.

I look closely at the image on my screen, it's not someone coming but someone leaving.

Oh no you don't, ghost. You're not getting away with this.

Chapter 4

POV Ghost

I close the oversized entryway door behind me with two bags of essentials in hand. I've successfully left the inside of the house without getting noticed.

Something captures my eyes at the bottom of the staircase. I slowly take step after step before it comes into view.

Blood, blood catches my eye first.

I'm puzzled, there's blood, broken glass, and a black gun with its magazine off to the side.

Who shot who?

My mind is at a loss of what had happened out here, who would shoot someone right outside of the house? We have special places for that sort of thing.

Forget that, I need to get out of here, I need to get to Arizona.

I briskly walk the rest of the way down the stairs replaying what happened only an hour or so ago.

I hated Millie, she made me look stupid in front of X. For the longest time I thought she worked here.

Adria hated her just as much as I did, she stole the man she most likely loved from under her.

We knew Hugo was coming here so we set up a plan to break Millie and X up. Adria came up with the idea and I executed it.

When X sent me to Columbia after our last meeting, I spoke with Hugo.

I betrayed X.

I hated X, he's a little shit that got handed the business on a silver platter that I worked my whole life for. I worked side by side with Emilio, X's father, we built this business together alongside Mateo, Julian's father. The three of us were successful and thriving. When Emilio's brother killed him, he didn't even see it coming, he was shot point blank in his sleep and I was regretfully happy until I found out all of this fucking work I put in got handed to a young little prick, X. I had to take orders from a man that could be my son. I wanted him to pay. He fucking knew better than to fall in love, he made it so obvious like the naive little boy I knew he was. I told Hugo that X had been distracted by a girl, because he had, I wasn't lying. Adria, Hugo, and I jumped at that opportunity. The plan was to throw X off with Hugo coming early, Hugo would offer up his daughter demanding that he show her a good time and then I would be on watch-out duty, luring Millie out to witness just how shitty of a person X is.

All was going well and exactly as planned until Millie opened the door, clearly in X's clothing.

I astonished myself when I apologized to her for my actions. My plan was only to tell her that X couldn't find his phone and wanted me to escort her down to where he was but instead, I apologized to her.

We made it to room 314, she held the gold door knob in her hand looking overtaken with anxiety and that's when it hit me.

Remorse, guilt, and heartbreak.

I no longer saw Millie there, I saw my daughter.

My beautiful 21-year-old daughter, Gabrielle.

That's all I saw was her. What if that was Gabrielle ready to get her heartbroken by the man she loved, even if he was a piece of shit? The rare emotion of guilt washed over me and I pleaded for Millie to not open the door.

Anxiety, nervousness, fear, and curiosity won her over though. She opened the door, and she walked out with that new image in her mind. My heart broke for that girl who was nothing more than collateral damage and leverage to me only hours before. I saw this empty and numb young woman walk past me and although I wanted to apologize to her for my vile actions, sorry would mean next to nothing to her in that moment.

I dissipate my thoughts as I come closer to my car.

I keep my eyes on my white Chevy Tahoe, almost there, I take the handle in my hand ready to pull until I feel something pressed at the back of my head, a gun.

Chapter 5

POV X

Ghost freezes as soon as the gun touches his grimy, greasy skull.

"Where the fuck do you think you're goin..?" I spit out.

His rough cracked hands are on the handle of the white car.

"Slowly turn around with your hands in the air," I say full of power.

Thank fuck the gun was still laying on the asphalt just waiting to be used.

He ever so slowly removes his hand and guides both hands just on either side of his ears. I want to look this fucker in the eye when I send a bullet through that brainless head of his.

He looks behind me at the mess that was left not long ago because of him. My own guy fucking betrayed me.

"What did you do to her X?" He asks like a little bitch.

I laugh for a second and then immediately change my tone back to serious.

"Oh, now you're concerned about her? Now you care? You piece of shit fucking snake." I demand.

I bring the gun to his forehead and he doesn't move a single inch.

"Who else was in on this?" I ask hastily.

He pivots his dark, almost black eyes to the ground and closes his eyes. He doesn't want to be a snitch.

"What does it even fucking matter at this point Ghost? You know what happens next, we've done this plenty of times to others before." I say shrugging my shoulders as if it's a daily activity.

He stays quiet.

"Ugh," I grunt impatiently. "I'm waiting...who the fuck else was in on this? Snitch or not, your cell-less brain is going to be lying on the ground in about a minute anyway." I say matter of fact.

"Adria and Hugo" he quietly says with closed eyes.

"Yeah...that's what I thought," I say already assuming who but wanting it confirmed.

I click the safety off on the gun, ready to end this conniving fucker once and for all.

"Please X, I have a daughter." He whispers.

"Am I supposed to give a fuck?" I spit out.

What? The same daughter he basically abandoned twenty-some years ago and only sees a few times a year somewhere in the Vegas area? He should've thought of that before he fucked with me. I don't give a fuck if he has a daughter...

And something suddenly clicks in my head by that single word.

"A daughter."

"I have a daughter," I whisper.

I have a daughter.

It hits me like a ton of bricks at once.

"How could I be so fucking blind?" I ask myself.

"Uh...look X, I'm sorry I wanted to tell you for so long." Ghost says in a sympathetic tone.

"Shut the fuck up," I whisper out, thinking to myself.

How did I not know this sooner? No private investigator could know where Millie is but I do, I know where my girl is simply just by knowing her.

"Give me your keys" I speak at a louder volume than my previous statements.

"What?" Ghost asks confused with worry.

"Give me your keys and I'll let you see another day," I demand.

I put the safety back on the gun and lower it to my side impatiently waiting for Ghost's keys.

I snatch them out of his hand as soon as they are pulled from his pocket.

"Get the fuck out of my face and get the fuck out of my way, I never want to see you back here again," I say meaning it.

Chapter 6

POV Ghost

That was a close one in a couple of different ways.

I almost just got my head blown off and I almost admitted my real secret to him that I intend to take to the grave with me.

I watch X speed off, squealing my brand-new tires in my brand-new car.

"Fucker" I say to myself, shaking my head.

I don't know what sort of realization he just had and I don't care I just need to get the fuck out of here.

I walk back to the house getting my keys to the other car I have here.

Once I've retrieved them I take one last glance around the house, the home that I built with my now long-gone partners.

I get into my blue Corvette and bring the engine to life as it roars a sound I love. I exit from the tall black gate bring my arm out the window and extend my middle finger to the house. "Fuck you, Sunset Avenue," I say to no one but myself.

Plans have changed, I need to go off the grid, I can't go to Arizona anymore, there's not enough time.

Airport, I need to get to the airport.

I know X, he'll come after me eventually which is why Enzo told his girlfriend Stephanie, he was moving to Madrid, he didn't, he moved to a secret location 6ft under after betraying X for something.

I pull out my cell phone to call Gabrielle, no answer. It's still early so she's probably sleeping. I call Gina instead, and she answers by the third ring.

"What is it Ghost?" She asks annoyed through the line.

"I need to talk to Gabrielle," I explain.

"She's sleeping." She says.

"Wake her up!" I demand.

"Ugh, what happened now?" She asks in the same tone.

Jesus Gina, she annoys the hell out of me sometimes. At one point I loved her the way X loves Millie. She was a married woman but our connection with one another was undeniable. We'd sneak off together when her husband was away on business. One day she told me she fell pregnant, which is now a beautiful Gabrielle. Her husband would've killed us had he known, so she packed up and left. I visited her from time to time and gave her money to get by. Eventually, things just couldn't work out in our favor and our secret relationship ended. She found another man a few years later and lives a boring conventional life now with another two kids. She's become a bitchy old hag, still a goddamn goddess but a bitch that hates when I come around.

"Just get her on the phone." I spit out.

"No, tell me right now." She demands.

"I need to leave the country, I have to go into hiding Gina," I explain in one breath.

"So today's the day huh, I guess they don't call you Ghost for nothing." She says almost in a humorous tone.

"I'll get her, but answer me this, who'd you piss off that badly that you need to leave the country?" She asks curiously.

"Your son"

Chapter 7

POV Millie

My fingers delicately graze the bright green grass as the morning dew coats my fingers as I sit full of depression cross-legged on the ground. I arrived twenty minutes ago, just after sunrise.

I let out a loud exhale and succumbed to my depressive state, letting tears fall in a stream down my face for the first time since I left.

I pointlessly wipe away continuous tears with X's black hoodie that I'm still wearing. It smells like him which makes me cry even harder.

"Mama" I cry out to the headstone in front of me.

"I wish you were here, I really need you right now," I whisper through sobs.

"I need you to tell me what to do, I need your guidance mom, I'm so freaking alone." I stare at the glossed stone through blurry eyes.

What am I going to do? I'm completely at square one, once again. I need to figure out what is going to happen for the next two weeks. I can afford a motel or hotel now luckily, but should I stay in San Diego or Los Angeles?

I need a new phone.

Now that time has passed, I don't know what possessed me to smash my phone and point a gun at X and Julian.

Oh god, I'm psychotic.

I was so desperate to leave I just did whatever I could to do at the time. I'd never take another life, not intentionally at least.

The image of X with those whores is making my stomach hurt and my heart clench. I'll never be able to get over that. How could he do that to me? To us? I knew deep down nothing good could've come from this past weekend.

Right now, I should be snuggled in X's warm bed while he holds me in his arms. My head is so jumbled I still can't process it all, I have so many unanswered questions.

Was he going to just climb into bed with me and act as though nothing ever happened?

The betrayal..

Tears continue to pour out of my eyes, I hate him so fucking much but a part of me still loves him for who he is and not what he's done. I can't forgive him though, I can't just move on from this, not today, not tomorrow, not ever.

I close my eyes hugging my knees to my chest with my head tucked in, the beautiful scent of X takes over my nostrils again as my face makes contact with the cotton. I'm crying so hard I can barely catch my breath. I move my hands to my head tugging at the roots when I suddenly feel a hand over mine and a head resting on my shoulder.

Chapter 8

POV Millie

My fingers delicately graze the bright green grass as the morning dew coats my fingers as I sit full of depression cross-legged on the ground. I arrived twenty minutes ago, just after sunrise.

I let out a loud exhale and succumbed to my depressive state, letting tears fall in a stream down my face for the first time since I left.

I pointlessly wipe away continuous tears with X's black hoodie that I'm still wearing. It smells like him which makes me cry even harder.

"Mama" I cry out to the headstone in front of me.

"I wish you were here, I really need you right now," I whisper through sobs.

"I need you to tell me what to do, I need your guidance mom, I'm so freaking alone." I stare at the glossed stone through blurry eyes.

What am I going to do? I'm completely at square one, once again. I need to figure out what is going to happen for the next two weeks. I can afford a motel or hotel now luckily, but should I stay in San Diego or Los Angeles?

I need a new phone.

Now that time has passed, I don't know what possessed me to smash my phone and point a gun at X and Julian.

Oh god, I'm psychotic.

I was so desperate to leave I just did whatever I could to do at the time. I'd never take another life, not intentionally at least.

The image of X with those whores is making my stomach hurt and my heart clench. I'll never be able to get over that. How could he do that to me? To us? I knew deep down nothing good could've come from this past weekend.

Right now, I should be snuggled in X's warm bed while he holds me in his arms. My head is so jumbled I still can't process it all, I have so many unanswered questions.

Was he going to just climb into bed with me and act as though nothing ever happened?

The betrayal..

Tears continue to pour out of my eyes, I hate him so fucking much but a part of me still loves him for who he is and not what he's done. I can't forgive him though, I can't just move on from this, not today, not tomorrow, not ever.

I close my eyes hugging my knees to my chest with my head tucked in, the beautiful scent of X takes over my nostrils again as my face makes contact with the cotton. I'm crying so hard I can barely catch my breath. I move my hands to my head tugging at the roots when I suddenly feel a hand over mine and a head resting on my shoulder.

Chapter 9

I hop on Interstate 5 driving southbound to San Diego. I'm going as fast as I can without drawing attention to myself. Although I have cops who work for me on the inside, it's the rookie pricks who want a gold star that I need to watch out for the most.

Goddammit, I want to floor this son of bitch. Every minute feels like an hour, I need to get to her.

I love this girl and I know that anytime she's upset she calls her mom, well she's livid and heartbroken, doesn't exactly have a phone to call Mom so that of course would mean she's at the cemetery.

Fuck, I started driving without even knowing where I'm going, my one thought was San Diego but not where in San Diego.

I try to pull my phone from my pocket.

"Fuck!"

My hand is killing me and I just rubbed it against my pants. The friction of one another sends a searing pain all the way up my shoulder.

"Ray," I say through the phone.

"I'm sorry X, I'm still working on Miss Taylor's location, I need a bit more time," Ray explains.

"No, no, it's not that. I need you to find the location of where Millie's mom is buried, her name was Ellen Hill, you gave me a brief description of Ellen in Millie's investigation report, I just need to know where she's buried."

I say so fast I don't even know if he comprehended my words.

"Uh okay, sure..give me a minute and I can call you back," Ray says laced with confusion in his voice.

I keep my eyes focused on the road determined to get to my destination, my phone rings, Ray.

"Thank god," I say to myself.

"Where is it ray?"

He tells me the location and I type it into Google Maps as fast as my fucked up fingers will allow.

...

An hour later, I pull up to the front gates of the resting place of the deceased. My heart is hammering in my chest, she's so close.

I slowly drive through and see Millie's car alongside what I'm assuming is Mia's.

I park a little in the distance so I can't be noticed just yet.

I spot Millie and Stephanie sitting next to a grave which has to be Ellen's. My heart has seized at the image of the woman I love, she's still wearing my black hoodie.

She looks so distressed and I'm disgusted by myself, I caused this. I caused this pain for her.

I see Steph holding her while Millie is crying. I want to run out of this car and hug her but after my desperate attempts to find her and finally doing so, driving two hours to beg her for forgiveness, I can't.

I can't get out of this car.

I can't take a sacred place for her away and taint it with my presence.

So instead, I watch.

I watch the love of my life cry in the arms of her best friend as she consoles her. I hate myself, I hate who I am and what I've done.

I cover my face with my hands and run my fucked up hands through my hair, I'm filled with stress.

I look at Millie, only her back is visible, she's looking angry as Steph appears to be listening to what she's saying by nodding her head.

I want to hear what she's saying but it's impossible from here, that is until, my baby screams at the top of her lungs, audible for the whole state of California, "When is enough, enough?!"

I lose it. I absolutely fucking lose it.

I cry like a fucking baby alone in Ghost's car, slamming my already messed up hands into the steering wheel with force and then pushing and pulling at it.

I fucking did this.

"I'm so sorry Millie, I'm so so sorry," I cry to myself.

I want nothing more than to be the one holding her right now, consoling her, wiping tears away, I want to be the one she needs when she feels helpless and lost, I want to be the one to tell her everything will be okay.

But I can't, because I'm the one that did this and everything is not okay.

I take one last good look at my girl and drive away with tears running down my face.

Chapter 10

Three years of pent-up frustration and despair were just released. I couldn't hold it in for a second longer as it was boiling over uncontrollably, spewing like a volcano and the pressure has finally been set free.

Steph has tears falling rapidly from her eyes as mine have stopped.

My heart is still going a mile a minute from my breakdown, I inhale and exhale the warm California air into my lungs as I feeling a weight has been lifted.

"Okay, I'm done," I say to Steph.

She doesn't say anything, just grabs onto me tightly and cries.

"I'm sorry you felt this way in solidarity Emily, I'm so sorry, I should've been there for you more," She sobs.

"No Steph, I did this to myself, you have nothing to be sorry for," I explain, now consoling her, the two of us are an actual train wreck.

Steph wipes away her tears, "so now what?" She asks shrugging her shoulders.

"Well for starters, I need a new phone," I laugh, surprising myself.

"Yeah, I'll say," Steph says rolling her eyes.

"And I need to find a hotel or something, I'm gonna stay the night here in San Diego," I explain and she nods her head.

"I'll stay too," Steph demands.

I nod my head "Okay."

"Alright," I say standing up, "let's go then."

...

Because the cell phone store doesn't open until 9 am, a new phone is going to have to wait until later. What does it even matter? I'm with the only person in the world I need right now anyway.

We arrive at a nearby hotel that Steph insists on paying for, with an extra cost of extra early check-in.

After we're all checked in, we go to the room that we'll be sharing for the night. The hotel room is nothing like X's. It's just a standard room with two queen beds, a TV, a bathroom, and a few lamps that sit on small tables.

We're both overwhelmingly exhausted at this point from the lack of sleep, crying, and drama. The only thing we want and need at this point is sleep. I curl myself into the fetal position on one of the uncomfortable queen beds while Steph takes the other. I keep my back to her, while I silently cry myself to sleep, never taking X's hoodie off of me.

...

I wake up around 3 pm and my face feels as though it's burning and chapped from the salty tears. I groggily sit up rubbing my eyes, Steph is up and typing something away on her phone. She notices me and sets her phone down.

"Hey sleepy head, how are you feeling?" She asks hopeful.

"Wishing that the last 12 hours were just an awful nightmare?" I say quietly shrugging my shoulders.

She gives me a half smile "I know hun."

"Do you think I can use your phone?" I ask.

"Yeah, of course," she says handing me her iPhone.

"Thanks, I want to Facebook message my old neighbor Mr.Daniels, I promised his little girl I'd come back to visit and since I'm in San Diego, I figure I'll see them," I explain although she didn't ask.

"Makes sense," Steph says.

I log Steph out of her account and log myself into mine. I'm typing out a message when a text from Julian pops up at the top of her screen, I really don't mean to read it but the X in the message caught my eye.

Julian: it's going ok. X was a complete disaster when we got back up 2 the room. Never seen him like that, dunno where he went. How's Millie

My heart hurts reading that.

Where did he go? Why do I even care? Probably went to finish what he started with Aspen.

God that name just kills me now.

It takes everything in me not to cry again.

"Should we go get you a new phone now?" Steph asks.

I finish my message to Mr. Daniels and hand Steph her phone back.

"I think I'll just wait until tomorrow," I suggest.

She nods her head in agreement.

A few minutes pass and Steph tells me I have a Facebook message notification that popped up on her phone.

She hands me the phone, Mr. Daniels has messaged me back.

Hi Millie,

I think it would be very helpful if you came to see Isabella. She's been having a hard time lately. I think she may need a girl to talk to, something is bothering her and she won't tell me. She's not doing well in school anymore and the school counselor can't get her to talk either. She's always had a bond with you, can you see if you can get something out of her? I'm desperate at this point. I understand if you can't and just want to visit. We're free tonight or tomorrow night.

Poor Isabella, I'm not in much of a position to be giving any sort of heart-to-heart considering I'm the one in need lately but I'll sure as hell try to be there for her as best I can. It'd probably be good for me right now to fake happiness.

I send him a message back.

Of course, be there in an hour.

Chapter 11

POV

Millie

"Hey, Steph? I'm going to go see my old neighbors in about an hour," I say handing her phone back to her.

"Okay, sure. I think I'll drop by my parent's house while you do that then." She explains.

I nod my head.

Ugh, I have nothing here! All of my stuff is still in the penthouse. I guess I'll have to go there in my current messy state.

...

After about 45 minutes of sitting mostly in silence with Steph in the hotel room, I decide it's time to head out.

We both walk down together to the cars.

I point to the car that Steph walks to, "Um, whose car is that..?" I ask.

"Mia's," she says proudly.

"She knows what happened?" I ask.

Steph shakes her head, "no."

...

I drive to my old apartment complex, making it there within ten minutes.

It's incredible really, a few weeks ago I hated this place and loved driving away from it with the intent of never returning.

As I drive into the complex parking lot, it really doesn't seem so bad.

Perspective.

Perspective is everything, something I once hated, honestly is a dream compared to the house that sits on Sunset Avenue.

I park my car in visitor parking, walk the distance to the entrance, and make my way up to apartment 512.

I reach Mr. Daniels's apartment door and give it a knock. I pray to the good lord that I don't accidentally cry like a baby in front of them.

"Pull yourself together Millie," I tell myself.

The door opens and Mr. Daniels stands on the other end.

He embraces me in a hug, "It's so good to see you again Millie! Thank you for coming, come on in!" He gestures.

I walk in behind him.

"Isabella!" Mr. Daniels calls out for his daughter.

"She's been hiding out in her room a lot," he explains with distress in his voice.

More sadness falls over me when he says that.

Isabella comes out, beautiful as ever but definitely has a shifted look on her once happy-go-lucky face.

She runs over to me when she spots me, "Millie!" She squeals.

"Hi Izzy, I missed you!" I say hugging her.

"I missed you too," she says in her little voice.

For the first time today, I actually smile and it's genuine. This is just what I needed.

"I think I'm going to go take a walk," Mr. Daniels says and I know that's the cue to pry his daughter for information.

"Take your time," I say.

I have no idea how to approach this situation. I'm not used to having a conversation with a child, let alone an apparent sad one.

"What do you wanna do?" I ask cheerfully, even though I'm not, due to my own circumstances.

She shrugs her shoulders.

Great start...

"Can you paint my nails?" She finally asks.

"Oh yeah, sure," I say scratching the back of my head.

"Okay, I'll go find my nail polish, stay here!" She says running away.

I awkwardly stand in the living room, I walk over to their sofa table alongside a wall. It's filled with pictures of family photos. Although I've never met Mrs. Daniels, I know the pretty woman in most of these photos is her. She had long dark hair with dark brown eyes, a beautiful jawline, and just overall naturally pretty, I definitely see her in Isabella.

I turn around and see Isabella with nail polish in hand.

"Ready?" I ask the six-year-old girl.

She nods her head.

We walk over to the kitchen table and she hands me the purple nail polish.

"What a pretty color!" I say before starting.

"Mhm," she hums.

I undo the top of the nail polish and begin with her thumb.

"So how's school?" I ask.

She shrugs her shoulders causing her hand to shift in the process. I wipe off the excess purple off her finger.

"It's okay, my dad always gets it on my finger when he does it too." She says so matter of fact.

I chuckle.

"Yeah, it's not really their thing huh?" I say.

She shakes her head.

"Libby's nails always look so good, her mom does them for her." She explains joylessly.

I involuntarily furrow my eyebrows.

"Who's Libby?" I ask.

"Just a girl in my class, she thinks I'm weird because I don't have a mom." She says embarrassed.

Ahh, there it is....

"Izzy, you have a mom," I say looking into big brown sad eyes.

Her demeanor suddenly changes to frustration, "well where is she? Daddy said she went to heaven and she still hasn't come back!" She lets out in one breath.

Oh my god.

This poor little girl. How long has she been wondering about her mother's return? How do you explain what death really is to a child?

Did X feel this way as a ten-year-old boy? Did he wonder every day when his mom would come back? My heart breaks for the once child that he was. I may hate him right now but in this moment my love is stronger.

"Isabella...your mommy..." I trail off not knowing how to phrase any of this.

I look down at her little hand taking it in mine.

"Isabella, I'm so sorry, but your mommy can't come back." I release the words that cut through my heart for this little girl.

"Why? Why does everyone else get to keep their moms but not me?" She looks at me with despair in her face.

"I don't know Isabella, some people, they don't have moms that can be with them and some people don't have dads that can be with them," I say as she looks down.

I'm really trying my absolute hardest not to cry.

"You wanna know a secret?" I ask her.

She nods her head slowly.

"I don't have my mom or my dad anymore," I say the words out loud and they sting.

"You don't?" She asks quietly.

I shake my head no.

"Did they go to heaven too?" She asks.

"Yeah, they did," I whisper.

"Millie?" The little girl asks.

She looks me in the eyes searching for answers, "will I always be sad?" she asks breaking down in tears.

Jesus, this is too much for me. I start crying too, I'm supposed to be making this girl feel better, yet we're both crying at the kitchen table.

"Come here," I say through tears extending my arms.

She walks over, sitting on my lap, and sobs.

And so do I.

"Have you ever talked to your dad about this, Izzy?" I ask trying to compose myself.

She shakes her little head against me.

"Why not? You can't hold all this in Isabella, I held it all in and it's not good, you need to talk to your dad." I softly explain.

"Sometimes, when my daddy thinks I'm sleeping, I hear him crying, I don't want to make him sad." She says in tears.

Fuck me, I can't do this.

"Sometimes, you need to be sad first to be happy again," I explain with tears in my eyes.

"But if I'm happy, will she think I don't love her anymore?" She asks.

I feel so devastated for this little girl. She's so young and confused about how to feel. For the last three years of my life, I felt alone. I grieved in silence just like Isabella and her father are. I wish I could take the pain away for them just as Steph and X wanted to take the pain away for me. I have been living in the past the way the Daniels and my father have. I've always been afraid to move forward, guilty to move on from what I've caused. Whenever I smile or laugh I instantly feel remorse for being happy. So I ask myself the same question Isabella just asked me. If I'm happy, will she think I don't love her? Will she think I don't miss her, if I'm happy would she look down on me with disappointment for the mistake I made?

No, simply no. She would be devastated for what I've been putting myself through. She would want me to be happy, she would want me to move on, and she would want me to take what she's taught me and carry it throughout my life. She'd want me to live my life.

I open my mouth to speak but Mr. Daniels appears out of nowhere and walks over to his daughter with tears in his eyes, I'm assuming her words had the same realization as mine, "No sweetheart, mommy would want us to be happy, I'm so sorry, I'm so sorry." He says taking his daughter into his arms and out of mine.

I stand up with tears in my eyes, rubbing my hands on their backs. She may not have a mom anymore, but she does have one hell of a dad.

Chapter 12

POV

Millie

I arrive back at the hotel room just after 6 pm and Steph isn't back yet.

I'm all alone again and with each passing minute without a distraction, I'm missing him. It's been 14 hours since I walked in on the most horrific scene. I hate that I miss someone who dares to do that to me. I replay some of the events in my head as I lay myself on the queen bed looking up at the white popcorn ceiling.

I love you

He actually told me he loves me, it was the very worst situation to tell someone you love them especially when your actions contradict your words.

Do I believe he loves me? Yeah..maybe..

Do I think he genuinely wanted to fuck Aspen? I don't know, not really but clearly this deal meant more to him than me.

Do I believe we can move past this one day? No, and that self conformation hurts like a bitch.

Although X is still alive, he may as well be dead. We will not talk anymore, we will not see each other, hug, kiss, or share each other's bodies again. Oh god. That part was so good though.

I need to mourn what we had and grieve what we didn't.

...

It's the official day after one of the worst days of my life.

Steph came back to the hotel forty minutes after I got back. We had some dinner, which I nitpicked at because my appetite has been nonexistent, we talked a little about what we did while we went our separate ways for those couple of hours and then I silently cried myself to sleep again. At some point in the middle of the night, I woke with overwhelming sadness, sobbed and Steph crawled into bed with me, holding me until I fell asleep again.

It's Monday, so Steph has to get going back to Los Angeles for work. Just the thought of her leaving and me being alone again tears a rip in my heart. I don't want to be alone right now.

"Okay baby girl, I gotta get going. Please, please come back to LA, we can get a hotel room together in the meantime." Steph suggests.

"Okay, yeah maybe we should, I'll call you when I get my new phone set up," I say before hugging her goodbye.

A few minutes later she leaves and I feel empty.

There are some things I need to do before I head back to the city of hell..like take a shower..

I get into the shower, the warm water falls over me delicately. I'm brought back to the day I showered with X. I don't even care about the sex part, it was the slippery connections of our bodies together that fills my mind. Tears fall down my cheeks and I'm unsure what is water and what are tears. I plant my palms on the white shower wall with my head down, "Why X? Why did you do this to us?" I ask myself through sobs.

...

After my much-needed shower, I put on X's hoodie, but only for a few minutes to run out to my car to get the blouse I bought a couple of weeks ago for my new job out of the trunk.

It's not ideal but what other choice do I have right now?

I go back up to the hotel room, change into my new light blue chiffon-like shirt on, and check out of the hotel.

I drive over to Verizon, when I get inside I'm greeted by a nice young man with brown curly hair, "what can I help you with miss?" He asks me, it's actually sort of funny because he looks much younger than me, calling me miss.

"I need a new phone," I say politely.

"Absolutely, come take a look at these." He guides me to an area filled with phones.

I pick one out, basically the same as my last. He rings me out and says "There you are, you're all set, is there anything else I can help you with today?" He asks and I'm about to say no.

"Actually, yes, there's one more thing."

...

I drop by a local grocery store and pick out a small bouquet of mixed flowers to bring to my mom's resting place before I head back to L.A.

I feel different today, I don't know if I feel free or regretful for making a rash decision.

I drive to the cemetery, I'm feeling nervous about what I need to do.

I park my car and walk over to the grave that I sent my mom in.

When I make it to her headstone I'm astonished.

The flowers I just picked out are put to shame. Someone beat me to it with at least 5 dozen roses of different colors. Red, yellow, pink, white, and coral surround my mother's grave. It's the most beautiful thing I've ever seen.

But the question is, who did this?

Chapter 13

POV

Millie

I sit myself down cross-legged on the soft green grass. I set my less-than-impressive bouquet of flowers down next to the beautiful white roses.

I'm in absolute awe right now by whoever did this for my mom, she totally deserves it.

The beautiful scenery is a perfect way to tell my mom what I came here to say.

"Mom?" I say as my voice breaks, great...I've gotten one single word out and I'm already on the verge of tears again.

I take a deep breath and exhale trying to compose myself.

"Mom," I say in a much more composed way.

"I need to talk to you about something. I don't know how to say this but just know I love you okay? Just know I will never forget you and the relationship we had, just know I'm sorry for what I did to you and just know I'll always carry you with me, but I need to let you go." I say and the tears come flowing as I knew they would when I said those heart wrench words out loud.

"You wouldn't want this for me. You didn't give me life so I could stop it on my own. I know you would want me to continue on, you would want me to be happy and to stop blaming myself for everything that happened that day. I know you, and I know you would appreciate it when I say, I disconnected your phone today. I need to let you rest in peace now, I'll be okay, whatever life throws at me Mom, I will be okay." I finish my speech as my face is covered with more tears, but not sad ones this time.

I wipe the remnants of tears away and I have no idea if it's a coincidence or not but the lightest amount of wind runs past my face and through my hair. Believer or not, but I'm claiming that as a sign from my mom.

I feel a weight lifted and although I'll always come to visit my mom from time to time I can't keep her in the in-between for me.

It's time to start my journey back to Los Angeles and deal with my misfortunes head-on.

Before I go to stand up, I grab the red roses that sit directly in from of my mom's headstone to let the beautiful scent fill my nostrils. I go to set them back down in their original spot but my eye is caught on something, lying beneath the red roses was a napkin with something written on it.

I immediately grab it, bringing the white napkin closer to my eyes. It's written in another language and I have no idea what it says.

I hurriedly grab my new phone and type in Google Translate. I need to know what this says. My first assumption will be Spanish.

I type in the message:

"estarías tan orgulloso"

It translates:

You'd be so proud

Oh. My. God, X?

My heart halts and accelerates at the same time, I can feel it in my ears. I'm so dumbfounded right now. It was X?

X, was here?

Chapter 14

POV

    X

I am just now pulling into the house after my two-hour drive back from San Diego.

Earlier this morning, I went to a flower shop and bought some flowers for Millie's mom. I know Millie will probably never know about the flowers or the note but honestly, it wasn't for her to see. It was an appreciation to her mother for raising the love of my life.

I don't know where Millie and Stephanie stayed last night or even if they stayed in San Diego last night but I slept in that prick, Ghost's truck in a nearby parking lot of the cemetery. I was so exhausted from the lack of sleep, drugs, alcohol, driving and just everything this past weekend brought on.

My hands are still so fucked up that I need to get Evelyn back over here later to get the rest of the glass out. As soon as I had that camera notification come up on my phone yesterday morning, I booked it out of Julian's place leaving Evelyn in some serious confusion.

By now, Evelyn is used to our antics. She gets paid well to not question anything and just do what she's told.

Now that money is on my mind, I need to secretly find a way to pay for Millie to stay somewhere. I've always had more than enough money to just blow on whatever the fuck I wanted. I could've offered a long ass time ago to pay for a motel or hotel for Millie to stay at the second she told me about her financial struggles but I purposely didn't. I wanted her to stay with me.

Right now though, I'm positive she'd never step foot back in this house so trapping her here isn't an option like it once was.

The dreaded walk up to my penthouse has my mind filled with the memories of Millie and me. I need to do this eventually though.

I open my door and see wine bottles neatly placed on the side of the countertops. My heart is already pounding with sadness.

There's obviously work to be done but fuck it. I just want to be alone with my thoughts today. I need to figure out a way to get Millie back, I'm not giving up on this, on her, the way everyone else did.

I walk over to my room and take a deep breath before opening my door.

I walk in and the black covers are pulled back from a couple of nights ago when she laid in here last, alone, while I was downstairs giving the wrong girl attention. I lay myself on the bed wishing she was here with me. It smells like her still and it's killing me, I want my girl back.

I take my gun, the gun that Millie pointed directly at my face, and open my bedside drawer to put it back in its original place.

A note?

There's a note sitting where the gun usually sits.

X, if something happens to me, just know I love you.

Fuck! Fuck me!

I fucking lose it, tears fall down my face at the note that my baby wrote.

Just know I love you.

What the fuck is wrong with me?!

I need to find her. I need to make this right, even if she never wants to be with me again I need to apologize to her and let her be happy whether it's with me or someone else.

Someone else..no fuck that. Whether it's with me or no one else.

Just the thought of Millie being with someone else kills me, I can't even fucking imagine how she must've felt seeing me with not only one but three other girls that she despises. I feel sick to my stomach for being such a fucking idiot.

As if my mind is read, I get a call from Ray.

"What is it, Ray?" I ask intrigued.

"Hey X, good news, I have been able to track Emily's phone, she's currently driving towards Los Angeles." He explains.

I look down at my hand that still contains some of Millie's phone in it, she got a new phone? Thank god.

"Okay, when she stops, let me know where she is," I say and hang up.

I'm feeling slightly better knowing I can track her down and try to talk to her soon.

I get into the shower, I need to look my absolute best for when I show up unannounced to wherever Millie ends up going. When I'm out of the way too needed shower, I throw some product in my hair and put on my most expensive cologne that I know she loves. I pull on a pair of black jeans and a dark gray T-shirt.

I get a call from Ray just as I'm putting on my silver watch, he explains that she's at a nearby motel. I look it up on my phone.

Nope..that shit ain't gonna work, I'm not having my girl stay in some cheap dump for two weeks with only god knows what kind of people are staying there.

Not fucking happening.

I start walking towards the front door until I hear a knock on the other side.

Ugh great..I have a mission I'm on right now, everything else can wait.

I open the door and...."what the fuck...?" I ask stunned.

Chapter 15

POV

X

"Mom?" I ask in complete shock.

She looks the same, only a little older than I last remembered.

"Hi Xavier," she says, I haven't heard that voice in twenty years.

"Wha..what are you doing here?" I ask.

"Can I come in?" She asks looking over my shoulder.

I really just want to slam the door in her face and say fuck you but curiosity is getting the better of me.

"Uh, okay," I say moving out of the way so she could come inside.

"Wow, look at this place! It's beautiful." She says looking around.

"And look at you, all grown up and so handsome," she says touching my forearm.

"Yeah..." I say still in a confused state of mind.

"We should talk," she says pointing to my black leather couch.

I don't know what my feelings are right now but I sit down as she suggests.

Now that we're both sitting, she begins to talk, "I'm sorry Xavier," she says looking down.

"I don't need your sorry's, it's a little too late for that," I say matter of fact.

"Fair enough.." she says with her hands clasped together on her lap.

She builds some confidence and looks me in the eye with the same green eyes as mine.

"Look, I think it's about time you knew the truth," she says gently.

The truth? Now?

"Go on..." I say impatiently.

"When I left twenty one years ago, it wasn't because I wanted to leave...to leave you. You see, your dad was an awful man, he was never around, he would fool around with so many different women and I fell in love with someone else, someone here."

What the fuck? She's really got my attention now.

"I fell pregnant with this man and I needed to get out of here before anyone found out. I moved to Arizona to be near my family. Your father would've killed me and the other man." She explains and I'm dumbfounded.

"And what about me...?" I ask getting heated.

"Ugh, well if I took you with me, your father would have come looking, but if I left by myself then I know he wouldn't." She says.

"Who got you pregnant?" I ask with extreme curiosity.

"Ghost," she says quietly.

I actually laugh at loud.

This has to be some sort of sick joke.

"I actually have a proposition for you," she says with enhanced confidence. She can't be fucking serious.

I raise an eyebrow but say nothing.

"I talked to Ghost yesterday morning, I know where he's going. I'll give you his location for twenty thousand dollars." The words actually come out of her snaky mouth.

I can't even fathom that she had the audacity to come here, give me a half-ass apology, tell me she had a relationship with Ghost of all people, and ask for twenty grand to snitch on his location.

"You're a fucking coward," I spit out and she puts her head down.

"I know you left for Arizona, I know you have three other kids, I know you got married and are living the fucking life as you left me here to fend for my fucking self! You know, I used to stay awake at night wondering if it was something I did to make you leave..was I not enough? Did I do something wrong? No. No, the fuck I didn't. It was you, you were the fucking coward that left a ten-year-old boy to a pack of wolves." I yell out in hurtful frustration.

"You got yourself into that mess and you weren't strong enough to face the consequences. Ya know, there are some people out there that long to have children and can't, there are people out there that would take a bullet for their children without a second thought, there are people out there that would protect their children at all costs and do anything for them, and then, there's you." I say the last part with calming hate to the woman in front of me.

"Xavier..." she trails off.

"No, I don't want to hear it," I say putting my hand up to stop her with whatever nonsense she's about to feed me.

"You know Gina, you almost had me fooled, you really did. I thought you came here to apologize for the piece of shit mother you were but all you did was confirm what a piece of shit person you are. So let me get this straight, you want twenty grand from me to give up Ghosts location? You want me to take the father of your child away, the parent that clearly gives more of a shit about her than you do? For money?" I ask hastily.

She keeps her head down with whatever emotion she's feeling.

"I'm not going after ghost whether you ask me for a penny or you just willingly tell me. Ghost may have betrayed me but what I've done is on me, betrayed or not." I say and she visibly looks disappointed.

"I'll do you one better Gina, I'll make a deal with you, I'll give you the twenty grand, shit, let's make it twenty-five. I will give you twenty-five thousand dollars if you never come near me again."

She lifts her head to meet my eyes, "Okay, deal." She says quietly.

"Yeah, I thought you might say that." I chuckle in disbelief.

Chapter 16

POV

Millie

I'm finally back in Los Angeles after spending way too much time with myself without enough distractions in the car.

I pull up into the motel that I reserved for the next two weeks. I intend to contact my new boss Marlene to see if she'd be willing to take me sooner to start working. Originally, I wanted to take some time for myself, get my ducks in a row, move into my new apartment, take a week, and move things in. Of course, life doesn't care to go as planned and it's in my best interest to just start working already.

This motel is a dump but it's only temporary. Luckily, Steph will be staying with me starting tomorrow. I just need to make it another day alone and hopefully not get myself into any trouble with the shady people walking around this place.

When I'm finished checking in with the creepy front desk guy, I go find my room.

"Room 12," I say to myself looking at the rusted out number on the door.

I get in and oh boy.

"It's only two weeks, it's only temporary," I say to myself.

The carpet is maroon with stains, there are two queen beds with a thin flowery comforter. The lamps are dim and it gives a creepy vibe. This room reminds me of one you'd see in a movie where someone gets murdered.

Shit, don't think about that right now.

I clear those thoughts away, I need Steph to bring my stuff here as soon as possible, maybe I can meet her somewhere to retrieve them.

I hear a ding in the right pocket of my denim shorts.

Please don't be X, please don't be X.

Chase. Thank fuck.

Hey Millie, are you mad at me? You haven't been responding to my texts. Are you okay?

Shit. He's probably been worried sick.

Hi chase! Yes, sorry. I was without a phone until today. I promise I'm okay.

Since I have my phone in my hands, I decide to e-mail Marlene for my earlier start date request.

...

It's 5 pm when I hear a soft knock at the door and my whole stomach drops. I'm not expecting anyone and the people around here don't look very trusting.

I ever so slowly open the door.

"Nope!" I say closing it but his arm blocks me from doing so.

"Millie, wait!" X says.

"No, I can't do this, not right now X," I say feeling overwhelmed by many emotions.

Why the hell does he look like he just walked out of a damn magazine?

I do not have the emotional strength for this right now. He's using all the tricks up his sleeve just in his presence alone. There's not a hair out of place, his clothing is fitting as if it was made just for him, which is possible actually, and he's wearing black sunglasses. He looks like a goddamn model, it almost makes me forget that I hate him.

"Millie, please just one minute!" He begs.

"No X, now move out of the way," I say sternly.

"I'm desperate right now Millie, you know me, you know I never meant to hurt you, I love you." He says as those words cut right through me.

"No X, I don't, I don't know you, and as far as I'm concerned, you're nothing more than someone I used to know." I say and almost feel bad about it because he looks as though he's about to come undone.

"I....okay..." he says giving up.

"Okay," I say pushing his arm away and closing the door in his face.

I silently cry warm tears. Why does he still have such an effect on me? Why when I touched his arm to push it away did I feel on fire in the best possible way?

I hear a light tap on the door again.

"Go away, X," I say through the door.

"Millie, I just need someone to talk to," he says sounding defeated.

"Find someone else to talk to then," I say harshly.

"I don't want to," he says with the same tone.

"Well that's not my problem," I say feeling sort of bad.

"I know, I just didn't want to talk about it with anyone but you," he says.

I stay quiet, I don't know what else to say.

"Millie?" He asks with a broken voice, is he crying?

"She came to see me today, my mom came to see me today," he says and he's definitely crying.

Shit! Why am I so weak?

I open the door hastily and he flies down on his back and hits his head on the gross maroon carpet.

Chapter 17

POV

    X

"Ow!" I say as my head hits the floor and look up to Millie with my sunglasses still on.

"Oh..shit! I'm sorry I didn't know you were sitting against the door," she say sounding surprisingly too nice.

"Umm..I mean, good..you deserved that." She says more confidently putting her hands on her hips.

I inwardly smile to myself. My girl.

I sit up rubbing the back of my head on the part that I fell on and take off my sunglasses.

"I deserve a lot more than that baby," I say and she scrunches her eyebrows together.

I put my hands up in surrender, "sorry, habit." I say glumly.

Millie crosses her arms over he chest, damn those tanned legs look fucking beautiful from where I'm at.

She notices me checking her out, "X...focus." She says annoyed.

I sit my back against the door with my elbows resting on my thighs. I involuntarily bite at my cuticles as a nervous habit and look up to Millie who is staring at my hands.

"Jesus Christ X, your hands look awful!" Millie exclaims, although she's been trying to put on a hard edge, she too caring for all the unfamiliar hate.

I chuckle, "yeah, well it's nothing like the pain I have in here," I say pointing at my chest in seriousness.

She looks down to the ground and I'm unaware of what emotion I just poked at.

I let out a loud distressed sigh.

"So, yeah, my mom came to the house today to see me." I finally say.

"How did it go?" She asks gently.

"Bad, awful, and everything under that category," I say shrugging my shoulders.

She gives me a sympathetic look.

"What happened?" Millie asks genuinely wanting to know.

"Well, it stated off as an apology, which was fake as fuck. She told me the truth about why she left," I say putting my head down focusing my eyes on the nasty carpet.

"And?" Millie asks quietly.

I put my head back up to look at her and shrug my shoulders and chuckle.

"Ghost knocked her up twenty some years ago, she cowardly walked away from the life she once lived and started a new one as if the old one never occurred, me included." I say with sorrow laced in my tone.

"Ghost? Holy shit." She says just as surprised as I was only an hour ago.

"Yeah..." I say quietly.

"And then what happened?" She asks intently.

"And then I told her how shitty of a person she is and even after all that she had the balls to try to make me a deal." I say laughing in disbelief still.

"Oh no..what was the deal?" Millie asks emphatically.

"She offered me up Ghost's location for twenty grand." I say emotionless.

Her eyes grow wide.

"Oh god, X." She says with furrowed eyebrows and shaking her head slowly in disbelief that a mother would do that.

"I didn't and don't give a fuck about where Ghost is, I'm the one that fucked up in the equation. Yeah, he's a piece of shit, betraying asshole, but so am I." I say honestly.

Millie looks surprised by all of this and I don't blame her.

"Wow," she whispers.

"Mhm, so I gave her twenty five grand instead to never show her face again…" I say feeling depressed.

"And.. she accepted…" I say as unwanted, embarrassing tears fall down my face for the hundredth time.

"Oh my god, X," Millie says with tears in her eyes too. She kneels down on the floor in front of me and gently puts a hand on my forearm. The comfort of her touch makes my tears more intense. I'm so fucking emotional lately, I haven't cried since I was ten years old and now I just can't seem to stop.

"I'm sorry, I don't mean to make you cry too, I just really needed to talk to someone." I say trying to wipe humiliating tears away.

"X stop, it's okay, I'm so sorry it went that way," she says rubbing my arm and I so desperately just want to hug her and never let go but I don't want to push it.

I try to get myself to together the best I can after a minute of comfortable silence.

"You know I can't let you stay here right?" I finally say.

She looks around the disgusting motel and scrunches her nose.

"I booked you a nice hotel room for the next two weeks, five minutes here." I say.

She shakes her head way too fast, "no, no it's okay I'll be fine here, it's only temporary."

"Millie…" I say, "I'm not taking no for answer." I kindly demand.

"I can't let you pay two weeks of hotel fees for me." She says declining my offer.

"I'd pay a whole lot more for you, baby, it's really nothing." I say and she gives me a scolding look for using that word again.

"If I can give a woman I hate twenty five grand then I sure as fuck can pay for a hotel for a woman I love." I say and I know I just struck a chord with my words revealing a look of happiness attempted to be concealed by a look of indifference.

Chapter 18

POV

Millie

I hate this. I hate that he still has an effect on me and I hate that I still love him.

Those words that just came out of his mouth made my heart sink and my stomach flutter with butterflies. It's such an awful situation, being in love with someone that you just simply can't be with. What he did has gone past the point of no return for us.

I hurt for him, I hate that his mom did that to him, for all of the things she did to him. I may have ill will feeling towards this man but I don't wish him any of this. I don't wish this on anyone. He's clearly torn apart inside and for good reason but it killed me to see the evidence run down his face. I wanted to take that pain away for him, the way he wanted to take it away for me the night I told him about my mom's passing. We have a unique relationship each other but at the end of the day, we both want something that we just simply cannot achieve despite best efforts. I've really known this all along but I fought it, I fought against my own gut feelings, I wanted him more than all the warnings that surrounded me.

"Please Millie, just accept it. It's the least I can do for you." X says breaking me of my deep depressing thoughts.

I roll my eyes at him.

"I'll stay at the other hotel if you promise to get those disgusting, probably infected hands checked out." I say confidently.

"Deal." He says putting his hand out for me to shake.

"Ew, no." I say shaking my head grossed out.

He laughs and I freaking missed that sound.

"Fine, worth a try," he says shrugging his shoulders.

"The hotel is Hollywood Inn Suites by the way," he says in a less playful tone.

"Okay," I whisper.

He looks me dead in the eye and says "hey Millie?"

I search his green eyes for whatever it is he's going to say.

"For whatever it's worth, I really am sorry." He says with pain in his voice.

I nod my head, "I know," I say barely audible as we continue to look at each other.

He gives me a sad small smile, "I guess I'll let you get to it then," he says and lightly smacks his hands on his knees. He stands up and tucks his sunglasses in the neckline of his shirt and opens the door.

He's half in the room, half outside and pulls something out of his pocket before he leaves. He has a piece of paper tucked in between his middle and index finger.

"Thank you for the note." He says. "It meant everything to me, even if those words are no longer true."

I nod my head slowly as I remember writing it that night, the night I wish I could rewind to before the shift in my love life changed.

I reach into my own pocket holding up the napkin from my moms grave. "Thank you for this." I say shrugging my shoulders.

He nods his head, "I'll see you, Millie." He says and although I want to spit out some snarky remark to that, I don't.

The door closes behind him and I run my hands over my face feeling way too many emotions at once.

That was that. I need to move on with life, we had a good run, a short one at that but nonetheless a good one.

I appreciate that X booked me a nicer room in an actual hotel but I feel uneasy with the offer. I know it's nothing compared to what he just gave his mom but still, I feel awkward about the help, especially from him.

Since I have none of my things with me currently, I grab my phone from off the bed to type in the address to the hotel.

I have a new e-mail, it's Marlene.

She wrote out that I can start as early as tomorrow if I want and that for the rest of the week I'll be shadowing Nick.

Tomorrow it is, tomorrow I start my new beginnings.

Chapter 19

POV

X

I drive away from the shit motel feeling at peace with how the time spent with Millie went.

She has her guard up and understandably so. I fucked up and I have to pay the price for that.

My phone rings from the pocket of my jeans and silently pray it's Millie asking me to come back.

Nope, it's fucking Julian.

"What is it, Julian?" I ask harshly not even meaning it.

"Yo, Hugo is here and wants to talk to you," he says.

"Ugh great...okay I'll be there soon," I say annoyed.

"Julian, do me a solid, get Adria to the meeting too," I say sternly.

"Uh..you sure man?" He asks confused.

"Yeah I'm fucking sure," I say and hang up on him.

I pull up to the house, parking my car in the private garage. I get out, taking my time, and waking to the meeting room. I stand outside the door with my hand cradling the gold door knob.

Go time.

I open the door to see Hugo sitting in my chair again, his two guys on either side of him, Julian beside one of them and Adria looking nervous as fuck in the other.

"Hugo," I say as I pull a chair out and taking a seat.

He nods his head.

"What can I do you for?" I ask.

"I want to discuss this past weekend and our deal." He says rubbing his chin.

"Okay, let's get to it," I say impatiently.

"My daughter had a decent report until the last day, but because you showed your loyalty to me and did as she wished, I'll make you the deal."

Ha, I fucking knew it. I was being tested the whole fucking time.

"I only have one condition, you cannot be involved with that girl under any circumstances and I will the sign contract with you right now," he says picking up the pen in front of him.

I nod.

He extends his hand out for me to shake on the deal.

I stand up, keeping a straight face.

I lean over in front of his face instead and say, "Fuck you, Hugo."

He's shocked by my words as I knew he would be.

I sit back down in my chair and leaning myself back, bringing my feet up onto the table, crossing my legs at the ankle in an unprofessional manner.

I look down at my hands picking at my cuticles for fun as everyone is in complete shock unaware of what to say.

"You see Hugo, I know you've been testing me for whatever reason, let's call it loyalty as you just said." I shrug my shoulders, "I don't know, I don't care, but you are not my boss, you would've been a partnership, so my personal loyalty to you means shit. I wanted to impress you and make this deal so I did whatever bullshit you wanted me to even though it had nothing to do with the business. You're a piece of shit and you know it. You handed off your own daughter to test my loyalty and to see how high I'd jump when you asked. I became successful in this business before you and I'll be successful after you. So, Hugo, I thank you for showing me your true colors through all this. I decline a deal with you. I'd be a fucking idiot to partner with you. So with all due respect, get the fuck out of my house." I say removing my feet from the meeting room table and standing up.

"Oh and Adria, you're fired," I say cooly.

She looks shocked and frantic, she swiftly stands from her chair ready to say something but I dismiss whatever bullshit she was about to say. "Not a fucking word Adria, just be grateful I'm not putting a bullet through your conniving fucking head right now." I spit out as she sits back down.

Julian is completely stunned in his chair and I don't give a fuck about whatever is going through his mind right now, he knows in the long run this will be better for us.

I'm not working with a group that betrays me. Ghost and Adria are weeded out from the group and now Hugo could go fuck himself, he played dirty and when you play dirty you're left with a mess. I can't work with someone that sets me up.

I walk out of the room leaving them all in there. I feel a weight being lifted, I just dodge a bullet. I think my favorite part of the whole meeting was his request or more like demand for me to stay away from Millie.

I laugh to myself shaking my head as I walk through the hall, that'll never happen.

Chapter 20

POV

Millie

I make it up to my new room at the Hollywood Inn, when I open the door I'm astonished. X booked me a suite that must've cost a fortune. It looks like a high-end apartment, the place is huge. It has a beautiful kitchen with black countertops and all the appliances are also black and high-tech looking. Lights hang from the ceiling over the kitchen and it looks so cozy, definitely not a hotel vibe at all.

There are two bedrooms on either side of the room and in between is the living room that contains a gas fireplace, floor-to-ceiling stone, and a thick wooden mantle that a TV sits above. Everything in here screams expensive, I may not ever want to leave.

I know I shouldn't do this but I pull out my phone to text X.

Thank you

He texts me back almost immediately.

Anything for you

Ugh, why does he have to say that? Why couldn't he just say you're welcome or something more stale?

I set my phone on the counter and get myself showered and ready for my big day tomorrow. Thank the good lord I have my work outfits with me. I bought some makeup and essentials at the store on my way here so I'm good to go.

I lay in the king-sized, white comforter bed after my shower and cry myself to sleep from todays events. At this point, I don't think I'd be able to ever fall asleep again without the exhaustion of tears.

...

I wake up from my alarm at 7 am. Today is the day. I'm excited and nervous all at the same time.

I get myself ready, putting light makeup on and put a black pencil skirt on and a white blouse. I look professional and hope to make a good impression on everyone in the office.

I grab my phone and keys and walk down through the gorgeous lobby and to my gray Acura for my first day of work. I arrive at the office within ten minutes. I've been here twice before but it feels different pulling in being an actual employee now.

I walk in and walk up to the receptionist who is a girl probably around my age with pretty blonde hair and light brown eyes.

"How can I help you?" She asks.

"Hi, I'm Emily Hill, I'm supposed to be shadowing Nick today," I say.

"Oh yes! Marlene informed me yesterday, I'll call Nick over, just one sec." She says more cheerfully than before. She picks up the phone that sits on the desk to call Nick.

"He'll be right out." She informs me.

"Okay, thanks," I say appreciatively.

Oh, fuck...me...

The man who walks through the hall is a mix between Chase and X.

Please don't be Nick, please don't be Nick.

"Hey I'm Nick," the man says with a smooth voice.

This is bad.

Nick is gorgeous. He's wearing a white dress shirt that fits him like a glove and gray pants that are equally fitting to perfection. The sleeves of his white shirt are rolled up revealing multiple tattoos throughout his forearm. Why am I such a sucker for the bad-boy-looking type? He obviously doesn't compare to X but goddamn he's a close second.

I look up to meet his brown eyes, "I'm Emily or Millie," I say stupidly.

"Well it's nice to meet you, Emily or Millie," he says with humor in his tone.

I can't do this, I need to request to shadow someone else. I need an old man or female to follow around, not some distracting handsome man. I'll never learn a thing being in the same proximity of him.

I follow behind him to his office, my nerves have multiplied at this point. He pulls up a chair next to him and pats it, indicating me to sit.

I sit next to him as he points things out on his computer showing me various graphs. He smells divine, but still nothing like X.

I try to keep myself focused as the day goes on. I've managed to keep my hormones at bay and actually learned quite a bit from Nick. By the end of the day, I feel better about actually starting off on my own next week.

Before I leave Nick says, "It was a pleasure working with you today Emily or Millie, I'll see you tomorrow." He says so smoothly, it was a pleasure...shit get your mind out of the gutter Millie, I do not need to be getting myself involved with anyone else, especially from work at that.

I drive back to the hotel feeling accomplished with how today went. Steph will be coming by to stay with me in a couple of hours. I need to remind her about bringing my things tonight, so I make a mental note to text her when I get back.

When I get back to my room, I kick off my shoes and plop on the couch exhausted from all the mental work I did today. Luckily I haven't received any messages from X today but at the same time, I'm a little disappointed if I'm being honest with myself. I'm in a constant battle with myself on whether I want him to never speak to me again or if I want him to try to redeem himself.

The battle in my mind is too exhausting, I text Steph, asking her to do my dirty work by retrieving my bags before she comes. Better her than me to face X.

Chapter 21

POV

X

There's a knock at the penthouse door, who will it be now? Julian, Adria or Hugo?

I open the door and it's Stephanie.

Last person I'd expect to see knocking at my door, I figured she'd want to avoid me for the rest of her life.

"What'd up liar..?" I ask but in a slightly playful way. I'm not exactly happy that she lied to me but she did it for my girl. She was there for her when she needed her the most and I can't be bothered by that.

She rolls her eyes, "sorry." She says and I know she's not.

"I gotta pick up Millie's bags," she says.

I nod my head slightly. I knew this time was coming but I secretly wished it wouldn't, I wished Millie would come back and not be able to live a day without me but that would be naive of me to believe.

"I'll be right back," I say and walk away to retrieve Millie's belongings.

I walk into the bedroom and grab the handle of the two bags, praying they'll make their way back here again.

I walk back to Stephanie with discontent in each step, losing my previous humorous tone as I'm reminded of my shitty situation I brought upon myself.

She notices my shift in emotion, "give her time, X." She says laced with empathy.

"How much, Stephanie? It's been two days and I'm dying here. I can't get her out of my mind. Im not me anymore, I don't know how to make this right." I beg her for instructions.

"I don't know X, I can't tell you an exact date or time, you do what you feel is best, I only know your relationship on the surface, ya know?" Stephanie explains and it was no fucking help.

"Do you think she'll ever forgive me?" I ask hopeful.

"Do I think she'll forgive you? Yeah, I think she'll forgive you one day but do I think she'll put it all behind her and move forward with you?" She shrugs her shoulders indicating what I didn't want to know from the person that knows Millie best.

I nod feeling helpless and hand Stephanie the bags.

She takes them in her hands and says "hang in there" with a half smile and then leaves.

I'm left alone with my thoughts again that are no good for me. This is all too foreign for me, I can solve problems with ease when it comes to business but for my own love life, I have to idea where to even start. I don't want to give up on Millie, I love her. I've never loved anyone before whether it be romantically or in any other way. I can't let her slip away, it'll kill me.

My phone dings in the front pocket of my jeans.

Great...Adria...I knew this was coming.

Adria: We need to talk X

no we don't...

Me: What do you want...?

Adria: I can't lose this job. I'll do anything, I don't have anywhere to go.

Me: shoulda thought about that before you set me up. Millie didn't have anywhere to go either so I don't give a fuck, figure it out.

Adria: X please..I'm sorry

Me: fuck you and take Penelope when you go

I can't deal with this drama anymore, I feel like I'm back in high school even though I know I'm the root of it all.

I have more important shit to deal with, like how to get my girl back, I can't go another day without her. Every passing minute makes me miss her more than the last.

I can't believe she found the note I left for her mom. I had no intention of her seeing it, I figured it'd disintegrate in the rain and she'd never know I was there in the first place.

In a way, I'm happy she saw it, I want her to know that I am proud of her too and not just feeding her bullshit by saying it in a desperate attempt to get her back.

I need to call Evelyn to come finish up the rest of my hands, the pain is starting to take over me and I promised Millie if I took care of my hands that she'd accept me paying for the hotel.

Although I want to camp out in the hotel parking lot just get a glimpse of her whenever she leaves, I don't. I don't because I love her and she needs space and my needs are less important than hers.

Chapter 22

POV

Millie

Steph arrives with my bags in hand just after 7 o'clock. I'm curious about the interaction between her and X but I don't dare ask.

"Holy shit this place is incredible! How much did this have to cost him?!" Steph asks looking around at the beautiful suite.

"I don't know, I feel kinda bad about it though," I say feeling guilty.

"Oh god, don't! It's the least he could do." She says walking to the fireplace to get a better look at all the details.

"Yeah," I say quietly, just talking about him is hurting, and Steph notices.

"I'm sorry," she whispers.

"He's got it bad Mills, he's going through it too," Steph says as though she can read my mind.

"Mm." Is all I say praying she'll spill more.

"He's desperate for forgiveness," she says and it pulls at my heart.

"Well, he should've thought about that before he did what he did," I say crossing my arms over my chest and gaining attitude in the process.

"Girl, I know, say no more, if it were Julian I would've actually killed him." She says with a chuckle.

"What's going on with you and Julian by the way?" I ask curious about their relationship. I may be depressed about my own love life right now but I want Steph to succeed in hers.

"I don't know, we've spending more time together I guess, I still can't figure him out most days but I think I'm the only one he spends time with," she says obviously feeling guilty for her relationship being more successful than how mine was, I mean if a relationship is even what you can call it.

Steph walks over to the couch sprawling out enjoying the luxury of the suite and making it home by kicking off her shoes and pushing them to the ground with her feet. Her blob of blonde hair is taking over the arm of the couch while she basically becomes one with the couch.

"C'mon! Sit down," she demands.

"I didn't want to interrupt.." I say sarcastically.

She waves her hand in the air to stop my nonsense. I walk over and sit next to her feet where it contains the most room for me to sit.

"I need to know everything about your first day!" Steph says excitedly.

"It wasn't technically my first day, I was just shadowing someone," I say modestly.

"Oh whatever Miss technical..just tell me about it." She dismisses my point.

"It was good, I think I'll like it, Nick was great," I say and immediately regret my choice of words so I try to recover myself by talking about the actual job and not the heartthrob I'm shadowing.

Steph spins her finger in the air, "No, no, back up, who's Nick?" She asks full of annoying curiosity.

"No one, just the person I'm shadowing Steph.." I say trying to stay strong.

A huge grin fills her face.

"Tell me everything," she excitedly demands.

I roll my eyes at her unnecessary investigation.

"He's gorgeous. He's like a mix between Chase and X," I tell her.

She springs up into a sitting position, "holy shit girl! You're just stealing all the guys in L. A aren't you!?" She asks with pride.

"Oh god, no Steph. He's just eye candy is all, I'm not planning to get involved with anyone from work and especially not with anyone right now for that matter," I tell her and if I'm really being honest with myself, I don't think I'll ever truly move on from X. He was a once in a lifetime sort of love for me and anyone else would simply be second best, unfortunately, I was only second best to him.

Today is the first day I haven't talked to him. My mind is cheering but my heart is hurting. I know Steph says he's hurting too but I secretly miss him, I miss his presence, his scent, his touch, his voice, I miss everything down to his asshole remarks.

The highs and sudden lows are exhausting. I try to remember the grieving process with my mom. There were times of the day when I felt every emotion, there were points when I'd be sad all day and I'd get a minute of numbness that then brought on a force of pulling myself together until I no longer needed to force it every time. I will be able to move forward, I just need to take one step at a time until I achieve it.

Steph has picked up on my low of the night and scoots herself close to me, "you'll get through this Mills, you always do," she says putting her head on my shoulder for comfort.

"I don't want to just get through this Steph, I'm sick of living my life with just getting through," I say between my millionth tear.

"Baby girl, if you want him, you know where he is, I'll support you no matter what you choose to do." She says now looking at me.

"I know Steph, but I can't," I say wishing I would've chosen the alternative.

Chapter 23

POV

Millie

Wednesday morning.

Another morning of not waking up next to X. I silently cried myself to sleep for yet another night but it's a new day and it's time to put on a happy face for work.

I pull into the parking lot, doing a glance over at my makeup in the rearview mirror. Today, I decided to amp up the makeup only by a fraction from yesterday and straighten my hair which has picked up a little lightness from the sun's rays. Steph teased the hell out of me before leaving because of my extra effort in my appearance thinking it was all for Nick but it's not, it's for me. I feel as though when I look better, I feel better and any ounce of hope for achieving that I'll do.

I walk into the modern-style building and find my way to Nicks's office. I gently knock on the door waiting until he calls out for me to come in.

Shit, he looks better than yesterday.

His medium brown hair is slightly longer than X's overall. The light wave in his hair is pushed back with minimal product making the movement so desirable. He's wearing dark blue jeans and a white dress shirt with the sleeves rolled up exposing the tattoo on his forearm. It'll be another distraction of a day I just know it, in a way I'm not too upset about it this time around because it'll keep my mind off of X.

"How's it going Em?" Nick says looking at me for a second longer than usual.

I laugh, "Em?" I ask confused.

"Yeah, Emily or Millie, just easier to call you Em instead," he says with a raspy voice. Oh god stop saying my name in three different ways, this is dangerous for me.

I shrug my shoulders, "okay, Em it is," I say matter of fact. He can call me stupid and I'll still like the way it rolls off his tongue.

I sit next to him not wanting to be anywhere near his vicinity but I pull myself out of my silly thoughts and get to work with him.

I take a little break around 11 am to go get some coffee from the break room, I pull out my phone, and oh no, a text from X.

Hey Millie, heard you started your new job yesterday, so happy for you, know you'll kill it.

My whole atmosphere shifts after that text. I reread it over and over. I text him back

Thanks

I want to say more, I really do, but what am I supposed to say?

I miss the hell out of him but I can't attempt to move on if we still talk the way Chase and I do. That'll just never work, there was just too much passion between us to ever just be friends. The day I watched Chase at Barney's checking out the singer of his friend's band didn't bother me in the least but if I saw X doing that? No, I'd lose my shit. I guess what I saw this past weekend is nothing compared to him checking someone out but that's beside the point.

How was the first day?

Oh no, an open-ended question.

Good!

I see what he's doing but we can't just act like nothing ever happened. In reality, our relationship together just had a nuclear bomb go off on us and we're acting as though we can gently place a blanket over the mess and pretend it never happened. It can't work that way but I'll be civil with him because I can't carry the weight of hate anymore than I already have throughout my life.

I turn off my phone so I don't get any other messages from X that distract me more than I already am from work.

I grab Nick a coffee along with cream and sugar on the side.

I walk back to his office and he's currently on the phone so I set the coffee off to the side. He hangs up a minute later, "Sorry about that, that was the Santa Barbara location just figuring out the last-minute details with them." Nick explains.

I take a sip of my little too-warm coffee, "about what?" I ask curiously.

"About my transfer," he says as if it were obvious to the world.

"You're transferring to the Santa Barbara location, when?" I ask looking into his brown eyes.

"Next week, Marlene didn't tell you?" He asks with lifted brows.

"No, I mean we haven't talked all that much about anything other than me starting," I say.

He crosses his arms over his chest and leans back in his chair, "Well Em, in about a week from now, this office is yours." He says and I'm completely shocked and he sees that all over my face.

He laughs, "Don't go making all this too girly now, I've put in too much effort making this place look as boring as possible."

I smile and look around, it is quite plain but it's an office.

My soon-to-be office.

"I promise," I say with a big smile. It feels good to genuinely smile.

He takes a sip of the coffee I brought in without adding any of the extras.

"Ew.." I say when he puts the cup back down on the desk.

"What?" He asks nervously.

"Just black?" I ask with a scrunched face.

He chuckles, "Only way to drink it."

I shake my head, "Definitely not.." I say rolling my eyes.

He smiles just as big as I am and I feel a tremendous amount of guilt as if I'm doing something wrong, like I'm betraying X in a way. I need to remind myself that I'm not, he's the one at fault in the equation and I can do whatever I damn well please.

Chapter 24

POV

X

I slap on a generous amount of ointment on my hands. Apparently, they're infected now which I sort of figured. I got a lecture from Slim's sister Evelyn on why you shouldn't keep foreign objects in your body. I wasn't fucking planning on keeping glass in their for the rest of my life, I had bigger issues to deal with, so yeah it got a little infected, big deal, I didn't need a lecture.

Julian will be here soon so we could talk about my "irrational decision" with Colombia. Don't give a fuck what anyone thinks about my decision, I'm not partnering with some deceiving prick.

I texted Millie earlier today and I almost wish I didn't. She was so short with me, she could've just been busy but I'd be naive to believe that, she was purposely doing it. Did she really not want to talk to me or was it a front? Either way, it hurt.

There's a knock on the door, I walk over and turn the handle.

I could punch Julian in the fucking face right now, he's here with Tank, Adria, and Penelope.

"No," I say starting to close the door on them but Julian stops me.

"X, we're just figuring shit out and then they'll all leave, I promise. If you don't want them in your house then let's go to the meeting room." Julian suggests.

I glare at him, "there's nothing to talk about," I say with an immense amount of anger.

Julian walks up closer to me and whispers in my ear, "Bro, they need to sign contracts before you let them leave."

I roll my eyes, he's right. I may hate him right now but he's always got my back.

"Okay, meeting room," I demand, no fucking way are these girls are coming into my place ever again, the only woman I'll allow is Millie.

We all walk down to the third floor together using the stairs, I know I'm going to have to write out some fat checks to get them to sign the nondisclosure contract. I don't care much about Penelope but Adria is going to hound me for every cent just like my mother did the other day. At this point, I'll give her a million dollars to leave me alone.

We get to the meeting room and I claim my seat again and everyone else gathers around to the open chairs around the table.

"You both need to sign nondisclosure agreements," I say flat out.

This is clearly all new to Penelope, she looks so lost which is more beneficial to me.

"X..please I'll do anything," Adria begs.

"Adria, the sight of you makes me sick, I don't want you here for another fucking minute," I say harshly.

She looks down hurt by my words but I don't give a fuck, she's a snake.

"I will do anything too, X," Penelope spits out.

"Penelope, this is a non-negotiable for you, you're out, I'll give you five grand to sign the contract and leave," I say firmly.

Adria knows Penelope could get a shit ton more from me and five grand is an insult but she keeps her mouth shut to be on my good side.

Penelope puts her head down looking upset and nods. She's so fucking replaceable, she should be happy I'm offering anything at all but she's been here a while now and knows too much to not be signing a contract.

Tank hands her the paperwork, she signs it and he escorts her out.

"Name your price Adria," I say chewing on the end of a ballpoint pen as Julian is sitting there awkwardly watching ready for the fight that will most likely go down.

"Nothing," she says folding her arms over her chest.

"This is my house too you guys," she adds in.

"It's not, it's mine and Julian's," I say looking to Julian for help.

"Yeah Adria, you have no ownership, you fucked up and you should just be grateful he's letting you walk away and with money," Julian tells her.

"Look, I'm sorry okay, I was jealous. Is that what you want to hear? Some random girl comes waltzing in and you just fall in love with her in like 20 days! You and I have had a history together for years and then you just tossed me to the side like I was nothing. You really hurt me X and I wanted to hurt you back. I didn't mean to screw up the Colombia deal, it went too far and I just wanted Emily gone." She says all way too fast.

I should tell her to fuck off but in a way she's right. I've known forever that Adria has strong feelings for me and I did toss her to the side the second I laid eyes on Millie. I want absolutely fucking nothing to do with Adria again but I feel slightly bad for the way I handled the whole situation. If I had just let Adria down easier then maybe Millie would still be here.

I look over to an awkward-looking Julian, "Julian, I want you to write this all down and then get it printed into a new contract." I say as awkward turns into confusion.

"Adria," I say looking over to her.

"I will let you stay under these conditions, you are only here to work. You will not talk to me, look at me, or come anywhere near me. If you have anything business-related to discuss, you will consult with Julian and he will bring it to me. If you break any of these agreements, there will be consequences. If you so much as stir up any more issues in this house you're out without any further discussion, are we clear?" I ask but it's really a demand.

She looks like she wants to fight off some of the things I've said but instead, she says, "Yeah, we're clear."

"Julian will get the new contract printed, in the meantime, you're done here, get out and I don't want to see your face again," I say meaning it.

She slowly stands up and keeps her head down losing every ounce of badass she once carried and leaves.

I don't know what possessed me to give her another chance here but I guess I empathized with her. My heart is broken too and I would do anything to get my girl back no matter what it took. Do I agree with anything she did in her attempts to get me back? Fuck no, but right now, more than ever, I get it.

Chapter 25

POV

Millie

I'm driving to the hotel from work feeling on cloud nine. I'm getting my own office? Already? I'm so excited and a bit nervous at the same time to take on such a big role already. Nick is a good teacher so if I keep my mind straight, I'll be fine. I felt a touch disappointed and relieved at the same time when he told me about his transfer. There's a definite connection between him and me, but one I don't want to pursue.

I pull into the hotel parking lot and walk through the lobby and into the elevator, when I make it up to my floor I get out ready to just become a vegetable for the rest of the night.

Oh... but how wrong I could be about that when I approach my room. My heart constricts at the sight of him.

X is sitting against the hotel door with his head leaning against it and his knees brought up. He's wearing the famous black hoodie with the hood up over his head and black cargo shorts. Why does he have to look so attractive without any effort? His green eyes make contact with me and I want to run away but that'd be a little silly.

"What do you want X?" I ask with attitude as if he has no effect on me.

He looks up at me as I stand over him.

"I can't do this anymore Millie, I can't go another day without you. I tried to give you space but I'm just dying here." He says desperately.

"That's not my problem X," I say in a too bitchy tone but I need to stay strong here.

He puts his head down, "I know," he whispers, "I just miss you."

I want to scream out I miss you too and run into his arms and forget everything he's done, but I can't.

I close my eyes trying to erase him from my presence, from the sadness on his beautiful face to the sadness on mine.

I open my eyes back up and his clearly infected hands are over his eyes.

"I'm sorry," he says with obvious meaning behind the words.

"Please, please tell me what I can do to make this right, I want you back, I want you more than the air I need to live Millie," he begs.

"I don't think there's anything that can be done X, I'm sorry," I say while breaking both of our hearts further.

He mournfully nods his head and stands up, he walks over to me moving my straightened hair away from my face, his touch makes my whole body ignite, betraying my mind in the process. He kisses my cheek while his hand gently cradles the back of my head and neck.

"I love you, Millie, please don't ever forget that." He says notably holding back tears and with that, he releases his lips from my cheek and his hand from my head and releases me in entirety, he turns his back to me without another word and walks away from me. I watch him take step after step, each one hurting more than the last until he can no longer be seen.

That's it, that's that.

The end, the end of Millie and X, and although I should feel freed and relieved, I don't. I feel significantly worse than ever before.

I slide my key card into the hotel door and wait for what feels like an eternity for the green light to come on, when it finally does I rush inside and get onto my hands and knees with previous held-back tears falling from my eyes and onto the dark wood floor. I can hardly catch my breath with the amount of heartache coursing through every inch of my body it's physically hurting.

Why did this have to happen, why?!

I loved him, I still do love him and I wish with everything in me that I didn't. I hate him, I hate that he did this to us, and I hate the inner battle I feel with myself every second of every day. I'm denying myself what I really want, I'm denying myself him. If I give in to him, I will be giving away my pride, and my self-worth for being a stupid girl but I'd be in denial if I didn't admit I want him more than anything, that I too, want him more than the air I need to live.

I pick myself off the floor needing nearly every muscle in my body to do so. I take a deep breath in and a hard exhale out and wipe the tears from my face as I sniffle.

I get into the shower washing away the pain of the day and when I get out Steph is on the couch scrolling through her phone. I wrap myself in a blanket and cuddle up to her.

"Another rough day, baby girl?" She asks sympathetically.

I nod my head into her arm.

"He came here," I say with depression in my words.

"X?" She asks surprised.

"Mhm," I hum out.

"Ugh" Steph grunts, "he needs to stop."

"He will, it's over." I cry again into Steph's arm.

She rubs my back, "I'm sorry Millie."

"Would a girls night tomorrow help out a bit? The girls are dying to see you but I've been telling them you need time." She explains.

"Yeah, I think that'd help," I say, grateful that my best friend knows what's best for me even when I don't.

My phone dings under the warm blanket.

It's an unknown number

Hey Em, it's Nick.

Oh no....

Chapter 26

POV

Julian

X hasn't left the penthouse all night despite all my efforts. We still need to discuss the deal with Hugo he blew off and losing his shit on him.

To be honest, I'd probably done the same thing. I'm not mad at X for telling him to fuck off because Hugo is an untrustworthy partner and we learned that the hard way.

Does it suck? Fuck yeah but in the long run, Hugo probably would've screwed us in some way.

I don't know what happened to X in the last couple of hours since the meeting with Adria and Penelope but he's deep in the dumps right now and I can't get through to him, he needs someone to talk to but he won't even let me in.

I text Steph to see if she knows anything.

Babe, do you know what's going on? I can't get X to talk to me, he's depressed as fuck.

I text X again

My man, you good? Let's have a drink

Steph texts me back

I guess X came to see Millie at the hotel and it didn't go well...for either of them.

Figured it was another let down for him.

I text Steph back

Alright babe I'll try to handle it here. I miss you, I'm paying you a visit to your office when you're here tomorrow

She replies with

Can't wait!

It sucks that Steph is away right now, I hate that she's been gone at the hotel and will be for the next week and a half.

X still hasn't texted me back so it's time to knock down his door. I grab a bottle of whiskey knowing we'll both need it.

I make it up to the penthouse and bang on the door.

Nothing.

Fuckin asshole..

"Open the door, X, I don't care if you're crying man just talk to me," I say getting more pissed every second that goes by without him opening the damn door.

I reach into my wallet, I've never had to do it but I pull out a keycard to the penthouse. X gave it to me years ago and it's just been sitting in a slot in my wallet since then and although I don't want to just walk in on him I'm desperate at this point.

I slide the card in and wait for the small circle to turn green. When it does, I push open the door ready to just let him fucking have it.

When I see him, I immediately pull my phone out of my pocket and fumble my fingers to call Slim.

After an agonizing two rings, he picks up.

"What's up, man?" Slim says on the other line.

"I need the Narcan, NOW!" I say in panic.

"Where to?" Slim asks in a now serious tone.

"The penthouse."

Chapter 27

POV

Millie

The text from Nick pulls me out of my depressed state and into a curious one. I text him back

Hey

I sit up with the blanket still wrapped around me and Steph is now texting on her phone too.

My phone dings again and I turn it on silent so Steph doesn't badger me about who I'm texting.

Nick: I have to go to Santa Barbara tomorrow, so I won't be in. You can either take the day off or make the office look less boring.

Me: hmm I think I'll decorate the office, hope you don't mind pink everywhere for your last week.

Nick: the way I feel about pink is the way you feel about black coffee

I giggle causing Steph to raise an eyebrow at me and then looks back to her phone. Steph probably thinks I'm crazy given my intense emotions.

I text Nick back,

Me: oh come on it's not that bad

Nick: it's worse than bad, Em

Me: you clearly have awful taste...

I actually don't care for pink but it's fun to mess around with him.

Steph stands up, "Uh hey I have to run to my car real quick, I'll be right back." She says sounding off.

"Okay do you want me to go with you, it's dark out," I say.

"No," she says way too quickly and walks out.

Okay...we're clearly both crazy right now..

I get another text from Nick,

Nick: hey, hey I do not

Me: okay sure...so what do you have to do in Santa Barbara tomorrow?

Nick: just signing new documents for the transfer, you can come tag along if you want.

Oh how badly I want to say yes to that.

Me: I have an office to redecorate remember?

Nick: lame

Me: sorry, shouldn't have left it so boring looking.

Nick: yeah, yeah. See you Friday Em

Me: see you Friday

Ugh, this guy. This guy needs to transfer like yesterday..he's going to make me do things I'll regret I just know it.

Steph walks into the room looking like she's just been crying.

"Steph! What's wrong?" I ask frantically.

"What? Nothing. I'm just getting my period soon so I'm emotional." She plays off.

"Emotional about what?" I investigate.

"I saw a homeless man digging through garbage.." she says.

Um..okay..it's LA, there are homeless people everywhere and yes it's very sad but since when does Steph cry over it? She's so used to it, I'm not going to push it though because she's pMSing and I cry about a lot less sad things when I'm PMSing than a homeless man.

"Okay..yeah that's pretty sad," I empathize.

"I'm gonna go to bed, it's been a long day and I'm tired, love you Mills," Steph says as she walks to her designated bedroom.

What the hell is going on?

Chapter 28

POV

Julian

I hang up with Slim and rush over to my lifeless appearing best friend.

He's sitting up on his black leather couch with his head back and arms out to the side with closed eyes. Foam sits at the corner of his mouth and his whole color looks off.

Please don't be dead.

In front of X on the coffee table lay pills...Oxy, a fallen-over bottle of liquor that is still dripping off of the coffee table and onto the floor dripping onto his feet, a white piece of paper lays besides the two.

I finally make it to him after my sprints and shake him praying he's just asleep.

"Wake up X, fuck...wake up!" I scream out.

"Don't you fucking do this to me, man, don't you fucking leave me!" I say in panic.

"Don't you fucking leave me...you asshole! Don't fucking do this man." I say as I vigorously shake his unresponsive body.

"Fuck!" I scream out with the unfamiliar sensation of tears running down my cheeks.

"You're my brother man, you can't leave me in this world alone. Please," I beg to the lifeless body of my best friend as tears run down my face and onto him.

The front door bangs through my pleads.

I jump off of X and sprint to the door opening it as fast as I can.

I quickly grab the Narcan from Slim's hand and run to my best friend to administer the opioid-reversing drug.

"Please god, please!" I say as look down at X for signs of life.

Still nothing.

"Evelyn is on her way over with a doctor," Slim breaks the silence.

"Fuck!" I whisper.

"Come on man," I say.

"Has it been long enough for another dose yet?" I ask to whoever is listening.

"Just do it," Tank says.

Green light. I give X another dose of Narcan, please fucking work.

We've all dealt with the incidents of an overdose with someone but this one hits fucking different. This is my brother in front of me right now. My normal logic to the situation is thrown out the window and replaced with panic.

I'm staring at X's neck for signs of breathing and I think I see movement.

"Come on X, get yourself out of this!" I say slapping his face with my hands to wake him.

He slightly tilts his head on his own.

"Oh my god! I think he's coming out of it!" I say and vomit spews out of X's mouth and onto his shoulder and to the leather couch.

At any other time, I'd be disgusted by vomit but in this instance I'm ecstatic.

"Fuck yeah, thank you god, get it out man," I cheer him on.

His eyes remain closed and moves his head to the side.

There's a frantic knock on the door.

Slim opens it up for his sister and the doctor, they rush over and I move out of the way to let them do their thing.

"How many doses have you given him so far?" Evelyn asks.

"2, The last one was about a minute and a half ago and he just threw up with some shallow breathing," I say in one breath.

"Okay, we'll take care of him, Julian, why don't you go get some fresh air," Evelyn says in a soft tone knowing the shit I just went through.

"Okay, yeah. I'll be back in a few, someone please call me if things go south." I half demand, half beg.

"We will man," Tank says giving a half smile.

I walk out of X's penthouse and go outside to ground level texting Steph as I go.

Call me asap, it's about X. Go somewhere where Millie can't hear you

I let out an overwhelmingly stressed breath and wait for Steph to call me.

Chapter 29

POV

Stephanie

I'm sitting with Millie on the couch as she's burrito wrapped in a blanket and on her phone looking surprisingly happy. This girl's emotions are all over the place lately, and I can hardly keep up.

I'm scrolling through TikTok when a text comes in from Julian.

Call me asap, it's about X. Go somewhere where Millie can't hear you

My heart instantly feels as though it has stopped.

What the fuck?

When it comes to X, it can be anything. I know tonight didn't go well for the two of them so I'm extremely nervous right now.

I tell Millie I need to run out to my car and when she offers to come with I immediately combat the offer. Whatever is happening with X, Julian doesn't want her to hear. I leave the suite with Millie inside and go outside to call Julian.

My heart is pounding through my ears as the ring continues until Julian's voice takes over after the third one.

"Babe?" Julian says through the phone.

"Yeah? What's going on Julian?" I ask nervously.

"It's X, Steph." He says with a raspy voice sounding like he was just crying maybe.

"What? What happened to X?" I ask dying for information.

"He overdosed Steph, he fucking overdosed on Oxys. He's okay, he's okay now he's getting looked at by Evelyn and a doctor but he fucking overdosed Steph, I found him." Julian says with obvious tears and now I'm crying too.

"What? No.." I say in disbelief.

"I fucking found him, he looked dead Steph, he was dying." He says and it breaks my heart that he found him, X is the closest person to him and he almost lost him.

"I wish I could be there with you Julian.." I say meaning the words.

"I know babe, me too, I really need you right now but you need to stay with Millie, she can't know what happened tonight, promise me." He says desperately.

"I promise Julian, I promise," I say.

"I have to go, babe, I need to check on him, I'll keep you updated." He says.

"Okay please do and I'm so sorry Julian," I say before we say our goodbyes.

Oh my god.

My heart is completely shattered by what Julian has just gone through, oh my god and Millie, the poor girl is completely in the dark about what happened and will stay there.

Her life is heartbreak after heartbreak these past few years.

How could X do this to her? To himself?

I pray he didn't purposely do this, I know he didn't do it to get her attention but I pray he didn't purposely do this to kill himself.

The thought makes me cry even harder.

Millie is upstairs right now going through her high of the day, I cannot tell her about X, she would be completely devastated and he's not out of the woods just yet either. Only three months ago she lost her father to a drug overdose and now this?

If Millie knew about X's overdose I don't think she'd ever recover, she's completely in love with this man whether she fights the feeling or not.

I need to go back up there before she gets suspicious and act like everything is fine when in fact everything is far from fine.

I get back up to the hotel room keeping my tears at bay, hopefully, any evidence has subsided.

I let myself in and she instantly notices.

Shit...

Hurry think of something!

I feed her some bullshit about pmsing and a homeless man, which I feel terrible about but it's the first thing that comes to my mind.

I don't think she really bought it but she's not pressing the matter. I tell her I'm going to bed and luckily escape without any other interrogations. I close the bedroom door and slide my body down to the floor and hold onto myself tightly letting a stream of tears run down my face.

X may be Julian's best friend, and X may be the love of Millie's life but X is also my friend and right now I'm hurting too.

Chapter 30

POV

X

I slowly wake up confused and with wetness on my skin.

Sweat?

"X?" I hear someone ask.

"Baby? Is that you?" I ask maybe out loud or maybe in my mind, I can't tell.

"No, it's Evelyn, I'm here with Dr. Adams, do you know where you are?" A girl says.

"Millie?" I ask out.

"No X, it's Evelyn, I need you to try to wake up a little more and focus on my questions the best you can okay?" I think Millie asks.

"Okay baby," I say.

I hear talking but can't make anything out, I fall back into comfortable sleep but I get slapped.

"What the fuck" I groggily say.

"X, man it's me Julian, wake up man, stay with us," I hear Julian say but it's hard to stay awake I just want to sleep.

"Xavier, I'm Dr. Adams, do you know what happened?" Some annoying man says too loudly.

My head is pounding and I just want to go back to sleep but people keeping talking to me.

"Go away" I manage to get out of my mouth.

"Millie come here," I say.

"Who is Millie?" The girl asks.

"You baby" I say.

"Millie is X's girlfriend or ex girlfriend, I don't know how to explain her anymore." I think Julian says.

"Ex girlfriend?" I ask while drifting back into sleep.

I get slapped again.

This time I wake up a little more than before.

"Would you stop?" I say to whoever slapped me and then close my eyes again.

"Xavier, it's important that you wake up," the loud man says again.

I try my hardest to wake up more so they'll get whatever they need from me and go away so I can sleep.

"Ugh," I grunt lazily.

"His vitals are okay, let's give him a few more minutes to snap out of it." Loud man says.

I drift off to sleep again and this time no one interrupts it.

I think I'm dreaming right now, I feel so at peace, I'm so happy and feel as light as a feather. I like this, I like the serenity that I'm feeling. I want to stay like this forev...

I gasp for air.

Pain, heaviness and hurting take over and the loud voices are back.

"Oh my god! Oh my god! Is he okay? You got him back? Fuck! What the fuck!" I hear Julian say, is he talking about me?

"Yes, he's back, he's back," loud man says.

My eyes feel as though they're sealed shut but I can hear everything around me.

"He's stable for now you guys but we need to keep a very close eye on him," the girl says.

"I'm going to make a phone call, if he wakes up I want to know immediately. I want to do an assessment for brain damage." Loud man says.

"Brain damage? Are you fucking kidding me? He could have brain damage?" Julian asks someone.

"I just want an assessment, it's common to be confused after an overdose but at the same time we did just lose him." The man says.

I overdosed?

Lost him?

I'm so confused right now and I can't seem to process anything, I try to open my eyes, I try to open my mouth to say something but nothing happens.

I try again, and again and again

"Mmm" is all I manage to get out.

Chapter 31

POV

Julian

He woke up.

He woke up confused as hell though, he thought Evelyn was Millie and it was fucking sad to watch.

I knew X was hurting but I didn't know the extent of it.

The room is a disaster, alcohol is still covering the table and the pills have disintegrated from the liquid. X is covered in his own vomit and sweating profusely.

The white note still lies there as the corners have now become wet and transparent. What does it say?

I pick it up as Evelyn and Dr. Adams try to get X to talk more.

X, if something happens to me, just know I love you.

This must be from Millie.

Poor girl doesn't even know what's happening to the guy she loves right now but it's for her own good.

X keeps going in and out of consciousness and it's freakin me out.

I don't know why I do it but I slap him to snap him out of it.

He wakes up a little more but only for a short time until he falls back into it and gains another slap.

Dr. Adams lets us all know that his vitals are okay and to let him come around on his own but boy was he wrong about that.

We gathered in a circle discussing his condition when X started seizing.

Dr. Adams and Evelyn laid him on the hardwood floor as he convulsed and then went completely limp and lifeless.

Tank, slim and I stood there completely helpless and overwhelmed with anxiety.

"Another dose Evelyn," Dr. Adams instructs.

Evelyn gives X another dose and then my worst fucking fears come to life, Dr. Adams is giving X CPR to a completely lifeless body, the body of my best fucking friend.

I pull at the roots of my hair overtaken with fear. He's dead, right now my brother is dead in front of me.

It must only be a minute of CPR but it was the longest minute of my existence.

Oh my god! Oh my god! Is he okay? Did you get him back? Fuck! What the fuck!" I say with complete relief.

"Yes, he's back, he's back," Dr. Adams says.

My best friend lies there still looking lifeless but the color in his face has returned.

Dr. Adams tells us he could have brain damage from all of this and it's killing me just as much as watching him lay dead.

I feel like I'm in a living nightmare right now and don't know what to do to move forward, I am useless in my efforts to help him.

Evelyn is closely monitoring him and out of nowhere it sounds like he's trying to say something.

"Mmm," he manages to get out.

I run over to his side, "c'mon man, get yourself out of this. You're stronger than this, you got this." I beg to him.

"Just give him some time, Julian," Evelyn says.

I can't wait any longer, this is torture.

Dr. Adams comes back in after his phone call.

"I'm going to have a neurologist come by here to check him out," he says to us all.

It's just bad news after bad news.

Dr. Adams sees the stress in all of our faces after his words.

"It's only a precaution you guys, I do believe he'll be fine, if he were in the hospital, which he should be, all of this would be performed regardless," he explains.

We all nod our heads in agreement to his request for the neurologist but I'm internally freaking out.

Evelyn breaks the tension in the room requesting a wet rag to clean him off of the contents of his stomach he released on himself.

We rush to her requests and I hand her a wet rag, she glides the rag along his neck and he shivers.

"Okay, that's a good sign, his body is responding." She says and I can finally let go of the breath I've been holding.

"I-I'm s-s-s or-rrr-y, mmm-mmm-il" X manages to get out.

I'm holding back tears of happiness for myself and I'm holding back tears of sadness for him.

"Maybe we should get her here? He clearly needs her.." Evelyn says looking down at X.

"No," I say shaking my head.

"She can't see this Evelyn, her dad died of an overdose three months ago, she can't know about this," I explain.

She nods her head and looks back down at X.

Evelyn continues to clean him off and there's a knock at the door, I open it and assume it's the neurologist.

Dr. Adams greets him and pulls him off to the side discussing something with him.

"Okay, hi everyone, I'm Dr. Fischer, I'm a neurologist and I'm just going to take a look at your friend Xavier." He says as he kneels next to X.

I'm so nervous right now.

He lifts X's eyelids one by one shining light in them.

"Good, good," he says, thank god.

He grabs onto X's hand.

"Xavier, I'm Dr. Fischer, if you can hear me squeeze my hand," the doctor instructs.

Thank fuck! I see X's hand lightly squeeze the doctor's and I can actually jump for joy right now.

Dr. Fischer does a few more tests and X responds to them.

Finally, good news.

The doctor comes over to us. "Neurologically he's fine, he's going to need to take it easy for the next couple of days, the confusion may last throughout the day tomorrow, he's going to be tired so allow him plenty of rest, his body has just gone through a lot. I want you guys to keep him well hydrated but I think he'll overcome this just fine." He explains to us.

We all agree to keep a close eye on him and Dr. Fischer leaves.

It's now been about an hour and X keeps trying to talk, since everything has physically improved with him, Dr. Adams leaves but requests Evelyn to keep an eye for another hour before leaving.

After that uneventful hour, Evelyn leaves. Slim, tank, and I pick up X and bring him to his bed to sleep it off.

I close the door behind me and clean up the mess of X's life and the living room for the next hour.

Chapter 32

POV

Stephanie

As soon as Millie leaves for the day I rush out the door to go back to the mansion.

She's completely clueless about what went down last night in the penthouse.

Julian had been texting me all night and into the early hours of the morning with god-awful updates.

I hardly got any sleep with the information I was receiving.

If Millie knew that they lost X for a minute she would be beside herself, honestly, I kind of am but I keep that to myself, I need to be strong for everyone around me.

I type in the entrance gate code and park Mia's car in her usual spot.

I practically run to the elevator to get to Julian and X.

When I reach the black penthouse door I knock impatiently dying to see them.

Julian opens the door and I run into his arms embracing him in a long comforting hug.

"I'm so sorry Julian," I say while stroking the back of his head.

"I'm just happy you're finally here babe, I really need you," he says and it breaks my heart that I couldn't be there for him last night.

I glance over my should and see X sitting on the black leather couch where all the shit from last night went down.

He's wearing a black hoodie and black basketball shorts with his body leaned against the couch and his hands in his lap, he catches my eyes and I just freaking lose it, I cry into Julian's arms like a big baby and I'm supposed to be the one comforting everyone here.

"It's okay babe, he's okay now," Julian says into my neck as he lightly kisses away my tears.

After a few seconds, Julian lets me go and I walk over to X, sitting next to him on the couch.

I meet his green eyes, "how are you?" I ask gently.

"I'm okay," X says sounding like he's lost his voice.

"Can I get you anything?" I ask.

He shakes his head.

"You really scared us, X," I say full of sadness.

"I know, I'm sorry," he says closing his eyes.

He leans his head deeper into the cushion of the couch and opens his eyes to the side to look at me.

"Does she know?" He asks cautiously.

I shake my head.

"Please don't tell her," he says and closes his eyes again.

"Okay, I won't," I say.

He runs his fingers through his hair, "I didn't do it on purpose, I fucked up." He says with his raspy voice.

"I know, X, I know," I say rubbing his arm.

"Alright man, you need more water, you sound like shit," Julian says walking over with a glass of water.

He hands it to X and he takes a sip but scrunches his face as if it were painful to swallow.

"I'm gonna go back to sleep, I'm so tired," X says and groggily tries to stand up but Julian holds him up by the arm and helps him up and they slowly walk over to X's room.

Julian comes out a minute later, "it's like taking care of a baby," he whispers.

I can't help but to smile at his remark.

He sits on the cold leather couch next to me and puts his arm around me, "what a fucking night," he finally says with an exhale of breath.

"I feel bad keeping this from Millie," I say looking up to Julian.

"I know babe, me too, but keeping it from her is to protect her, not hurt her." He says running his fingers through my hair.

"I know," I whisper.

Chapter 33

POV

Millie

I arrive at the office just after nine, I stopped at a resale shop on my way in.

It was a weird morning, I feel like Steph has been avoiding me. Women though, we do weird things when we're PMSing.

I brought in some small green plants, some landscape photos for the wall, and some cute pen holders. This should make the office look a little less...sad.

I set up some of the things, already significantly better in here. My phone dings on the dark wood desk. I retrieve it and it's Nick.

How's the decorating going? Everything pink already?

I chuckle at the message.

Me: Ha. Ha. No, I reconsidered last minute.

Nick: Thank you god

Me: How's the document signing going?

Nick: It's so much fun, equivalent to pink.

I laugh out loud.

Me: I'm really missing out then huh?

Nick: For sure. Would've been black coffee to me if you were here.

Oh shit..what do I even say to that?

Me: Sure..

Nick: Guess we'll never know will we?

Me: I guess not

Ugh, why does this feel so wrong? I mean it is..I'm flirting with my coworker but what feels even more wrong is that I feel bad that I'm flirting with someone that is not X.

I'm brought back to the memory of yesterday's encounter. He looked so sad and defeated but what was I supposed to do? I love the man, I don't want him to be hurt but he hurt me first and there are consequences to your actions.

Shit...what are the consequences going to be with Nick? He's an amazing guy and I think he likes me? I just don't want to get involved with anyone, I just don't want to get involved with anyone but X if I'm being honest with myself.

It's settled, single forever.

...

I make it back to the hotel around noon. I still have a lot of the day ahead of me with nothing to do.

Great.. alone with my thoughts.

Since I've been lacking sleep lately, I decide to take a nap before girls' night.

I, of course, cry myself to sleep before my nap.

...

I wake up and grab my phone from the nightstand, it's 2 pm.

I text Chase.

Me: Hey chase! Wanna meet up for coffee?

Chase: Yeah, sure! When?

Me: Whenever you have time

Chase: Okay wanna meet at Starbucks at 3? The one on Oceanfront Rd?

Me: Yeah see you then!

I freshen myself up, adding a few more curls to my hair since it flattened down from my nap, and touch up my makeup from the stream of tears.

I head out around 2:45 to meet up with Chase.

When I arrive at Starbucks, I walk inside and see Chase sitting at a table with his laptop in front of him.

"Hi, Chase!" I say with a smile.

"Millie, hey!" He says standing up to hug me.

I sit down across from him and he closes his laptop.

"How are you? How's the whole house thing going?" He asks.

"It's...not.." I say and he lifts an eyebrow.

"I'm staying at a hotel," I say embarrassed.

"Millie, what? Why didn't you tell me? You know you could've stayed with me again." He says all too fast.

Yeah...okay, not making that mistake again. Besides, X would probably kill him.

"Yeah I know, it's fine though. It's a nice hotel and Steph has been staying with me." I explain.

"Enough about me though, I'm totally fine, what's been going on with you? We haven't talked much since we saw Tate's band." I say remembering that night all too well. I mean it was only a week ago but it's the night X and I slept together.

Oh no, the thoughts flood my mind. What I would do just to sleep with him again. Stop it, Millie! Stop it!

"Yeah I know, well...I've kinda been hanging out with Jessie." He says shyly.

I smile, "who's Jessie..?" I ask.

He chuckles, "The singer from the band."

"Oh my god chasc!" I say laughing, "Good for you!"

He smiles and shrugs his shoulders.

"How's it going with your guy? He's not here is here? Ready to swing?" He asks looking around.

I put my head down and shake my head, twiddling my fingers together, "no," I whisper.

"The reason you left?" He asks softly.

I nod my head with it still being down.

"I'm sorry, Millie." He says.

"It's okay, Chase, I'm fine," I say lying to him.

Chapter 34

POV

Millie

I get back to the hotel around 5 pm after meeting up with Chase. I was hoping to get things off my mind but it backfired on me.

I'm happy for Chase, I'm happy that he and Jessie have been seeing each other but it makes me feel envious at the same time. I couldn't care less that Chase is seeing someone else, I care that everyone else in the world seems to be having a thriving relationship with someone and then there's me.

I need my girls to get me out of this rut I'm in.

Ten minutes later Steph comes walking through the door looking exhausted.

"You good?" I ask her.

"Hmm? Yeah. I'm great, why?" She asks.

"You look like a zombie right now Steph," I say.

"Gee thanks, Mills," she says rolling her eyes.

I laugh, "That's not what I meant."

"Yeah, yeah." She says.

"The girls should be here any minute, Mia can't come tonight she's on a date," Steph says.

"What?! With who?" I ask all excited but feeling sorry for myself at the same time.

"I don't know, some guy from online," she says.

I shrug my shoulders.

There's a knock on the door and I open it revealing Alina and Ellie.

"Millie!" They say hugging me.

"How are you, honey?" Alina asks me petting my hair.

"Heartbreak looks good on you," Ellie says.

"Uh..thanks..I think," I say confused.

"Oh my god Ellie, what is wrong with you?" Alina nudges her arm.

I laugh, I have a good sense of humor so I don't take it any other way than comical.

"Wow, this place is incredible!" Alina says looking around.

"Yeah.." I say quietly.

We all sit on the couch and I turn on the fireplace handing out red wine with glasses.

"How have you been holding up?" Ellie asks me.

I shrug my shoulders, "I'm not really," I say being honest.

Ellie rubs my leg in a comforting manner.

"I'm sorry," she whispers.

"Yeah Millie, me too, you know you can come back if you want, you won't have to see X," Alina says.

I swear you just can't have it all, Alina is drop-dead gorgeous but my god is she stupid sometimes.

"Yeah, no I'm not going back there Alina," I say while shaking my head.

"Why not? Ghost left, Penelope got fired and Adria is not allowed anywhere near X or she's fired too." Alina explains.

"What?" I ask so confused.

"X got rid of them, well, I heard Ghost left on his own but he'd be stupid to stick around." Ellie takes over.

What does it even matter at this point? What does it matter if Penelope stays, if Adria doesn't approach X? If Ghost is gone..what does any of this change? It changes nothing.

At the end of the day, it's X who fucked up. These girls are shittier than shit but when it comes down to it, any woman would jump at the opportunity to sleep with X, so no, I don't blame them, I blame him. His priorities were all wrong, that deal meant more to him than I did and that's what hurts the most. I was disposable through and through.

I excuse myself for a minute and make a phone call in my bedroom.

He picks up by the third ring.

"Hey, do you want to go out with me Saturday night?" I ask through the line.

"I'd love to," Nick says.

We hang up and I go back out to the girls who are looking confused.

Steph has been awfully quiet tonight I don't know what her deal is.

"You okay Millie? I'm sorry I brought it up," Ellie says.

"No Ellie, it's fine, besides, I'm going on a date with my hot new coworker on Saturday night," I say proudly.

Steph furrows her eyebrows like she's disappointed.

"Don't you think it might be too soon Mills? I mean it hasn't even been a week since you and X ended things." Steph finally speaks.

"So what?" I say in a snappy tone.

"Okay," Steph says giving up.

It's really awkward in the suite right now and this isn't going according to plan. It's supposed to be a fun night and it's turned into X taking over like it always freaking does.

I honestly don't know what possessed me to ask out Nick. I'm already feeling a little regretful about it as my anger starts to subside.

I should've been happy to hear about X getting rid of the rats but something in me just snapped. Alina and Ellie made him out to be a hero because he fired them. He's not the hero, he fucked up and he's still made out to be a god and it's frustrating the hell out of me.

"Enough about X you guys, he's dead to me," I say way too harshly.

Steph stands up and walks into her room crying.

What the fuck is going on?!

Chapter 35

As I lay in my bed, darkness is falling in the sky, darkness is falling on me.

I'm in physical and mental pain.

My throat hurts and my mouth is so dry, it hurts to swallow down water, it's almost not even worth it to try.

Julian hasn't left the penthouse all day and although I am grateful for him, I want him to just leave already.

I'm brought back to that thought of serenity I felt, I want it back.

I now know what it was, I was gone. I didn't mean to overdose, but god damn in a way I wish I didn't wake up to this life again.

I'm feeling lost, I lost Millie, I lost the mother I hoped for my whole life was a good person and was just scared of this harsh life in the mansion, but no, she left me for selfish reasons. I don't know what the hell I'm doing with my business anymore and I can't seem to get a grip on anything.

For a minute I had no worries, no pain, no problems. I will never attempt to achieve that feeling on my own again but it's something I'm currently longing for.

I know I fucked up with the alcohol and oxy, I know better than that I'm a fucking drug dealer, I know my shit but I was desperate to let go of the pain I felt for a short period and it just went too far.

I feel guilty that Julian found me. Julian and I are the closest to one another, it's always been that way. If the tables were turned I'd be devastated.

I think back to Millie and if she had known about what happened last night. She may not want anything to do with me anymore but that doesn't change the fact that she'd be devastated by the news. I just can't seem to do anything right. Her own father's life was succumbed by drugs and here I am doing the same.

I want to call Millie, just to hear her voice but I can't. I hate that I have to let her go but I need to oblige to what she wants and needs.

Julian knocks at the door.

"Yeah come in," I say.

"Hey man, you need anything?" He asks.

"A fat blunt?" I ask.

"Yeah, no you can't have that, my man," Julian says with a laugh.

"Hey man, uh I need to tell you somethin'.." he scratches the back of his head.

"What is it?" I ask with a sore throat.

"Uh I really don't want to tell you this, especially not right now, but Steph told me Millie is going on a date with someone on Saturday night, I just didn't want you to find out from someone else." He explains and the words cut through me like a fucking jagged knife.

"Wha..what?" I ask hoping his words hold no truth.

"I'm sorry man," he says carefully.

"It's fine, Julian, thanks for the heads up," I say.

"Do you want to talk about it?" He asks and I shake my head.

"Just go Julian," I say trying to hold myself together.

"I'll be in the living room," he says and walks out.

As soon as he leaves I rip the bedside lamp from the wall and with as much force as I can possibly handle at this point I throw it against the wall causing it to shatter, I take my glass of water, take a sip, and then chuck it against the floor.

I open my nightstand drawer, taking the note that Millie wrote me, I rip it up and I release it from my hands and onto the floor.

"Fuck you, Millie," I say meaning every word.

Chapter 36

POV

Julian

I don't even make it halfway down the hall when I hear things from X's room breaking.

I expected this.

I wanted to be the one to tell him because word travels fast in this house, half the house already knows about his overdose but no one is stupid enough to approach him, even if it were words of encouragement. X is a defensive person, he doesn't want anyone taking pity on him and he doesn't do well with kind words. X thrives off of the negative, he turns it into a challenge. X's dad formed him this way, just as mine did but my dad had a percentage more of a heart than X's. We were taught from adolescence to not let people in, to conceal our feelings and weaknesses, and to hide who we are as a person. In this business, you're a lethal robot. Millie is breaking X away from that and he's struggling beyond belief with it.

I don't trust X to have found this information out from someone else, he's irrational when he's upset, he doesn't know how to handle when things are out of his control and I want to be present in the case of him doing something he'll regret.

Right now he's taking his anger out on objects and not people so I'm satisfied with the coping mechanism. Had X found out from anyone but me, he'd kill the messenger in cold blood.

I'm not leaving this dude until his shit is back together and his emotions are in check.

The heartache he's experiencing is foreign to him and he's learning the hard way on how to handle it. I'm surprised as fuck that Millie is going out with someone already but maybe that's just how she copes, everyone is different. I believe Millie is not over X, not even by a fraction but if she needs to go out with someone else to deal with the pain she's experiencing then so be it.

I keep hearing glass break from the room and I hope he'll stop soon because he's going to overexert himself, but maybe that's not such a bad thing right now honestly.

I feel for him, it's just bad news after bad news for this guy, every day since Saturday night but at the same time he's doing all of this to himself, it's all self-inflicted.

I text Steph

Me: Told X, he's going off the deep end

Steph: Lovely..

Me: he had to know babe

Steph: I know, I know. Not really happy with Millie right now

Me: I get it but maybe it's just something she has to do to move on

Steph: yeah you're right

Me: miss you already

Steph: Me too xx

I set my phone down. When I see Steph next, I want to talk to her about moving in with me. I don't want anyone else other than her and I think she feels the same.

She better..or I'll be right where X is.

I feel bad thinking this, but thank god our relationship is nothing like X and Millie's.

Chapter 37

POV

Millie

I'm starting to feel bad about my outbursts of the evening. The tension in the suite is dense and it's all because of me.

I try to salvage the night by suggesting The Bachelor. They of course are down to watch but Steph is nonexistent, still in her room.

I really get to thinking while we watch an episode, all of these women fighting for one man. What makes him so special? Sure, he's handsome but when it comes down to it is he really worth it? Other than his good looks, which one of these girls is actually going to see him? To love him, to pick him up when he falls and pick her up in that same manner? When all is said and done, every single one of these girls but one will have their heart broken by this man. Why put yourself through that? All for the chance that he might choose you?

And the one.

The one that wins him over, what happens after that? He just dated dozens of women, made connections with them, had intimate moments with them while you were tucked warm in your bed thinking about him. What happens if the day after he picks you, he still has the other girl that didn't get chosen on his mind? Will he always wonder what if?

I sympathize with the others, because I am the other no matter what X says or even believes.

When Ellie and Alina leave I knock on Steph's door.

"Yeah, come in," she says from the other side of the wood.

I walk in and she's sitting on the bed with her phone in her hand. I sit beside her, cross legged just as she is.

"I'm sorry for being so snappy with you earlier," I say apologizing.

"It's fine," she says with her head down.

"What's going on Steph?" I ask in a more pleasing manner.

"Nothing mills, I just have a lot on my mind," she says falling back on the bed.

I match her position and lay next to her as we look up at the white vaulted ceiling.

"We can't both be depressed Steph, it was supposed to be my turn, you can have it next week." I say jokingly and she laughs.

"Sorry, I just wanted to join the party." She says with an exhale of breath.

"Did something happen with Julian?" I ask cautiously.

"Hmm, no, we're fine." She says.

"So then what is it?" I ask again.

"Nothing mills, just nothing," she says not wanting to let me in.

"Okay," I say giving up.

"Just trust me on this one mills," she says taking my hand in hers and squeezing it.

"Okay," I whisper.

I'm unbelievably curious now but I'll respect her wishes.

"Well I love you, I'm going to bed now, you know where I am if you need me," I say to my best friend.

"Love you too mills," she says as I walk out the door.

I go into my bedroom feeling extremely anxious about work tomorrow. When I called Nick, I wasnt thinking about the fact that I have to still work with him tomorrow, I just did it out of spite honestly. I mean do I like Nick? Yeah, but it'd never go anywhere. He's someone that deserves someone's full attention and I can't give him that right now, not while I'm still in love with someone else.

I really hope X doesn't find out about the casual date I'm going on in two days, he has a way of always knowing where I am or what I'm doing at a given time.

I lay in bed and for the first time in days, I don't cry myself to sleep.

Chapter 38

POV

Millie

It's now Friday morning and I dread having to go into work today to see Nick. I curl my hair, brushing it out after it's set. I do my makeup in neutral tones so it doesn't look like I'm trying to dress up for him today.

I walk out of the bedroom ready to go but still have a little time before I have to leave. I make myself a hot coffee. I don't add anything in, I take a sip of the black coffee.

"Yeah, no, not happening.." I say to myself with a scrunched face.

I grab the French vanilla coffee creamer out of the fridge, adding more than usual to dissipate the gross plain black coffee I had to force down my throat.

"So much better," I say to myself with a smile.

"Are you having a conversation with yourself mills?" Steph asks coming out of her room.

I laugh, "maybe..."

"Whatcha guys talking about?" She asks with a grin.

"Coffee," I say proudly.

"Well can Millie 1, ask Millie 2 to make me a cup while she's at it?" Steph asks sitting on a barstool.

"They say yes," I say with a wink. Ugh, why did I just wink? It brings me right back to Adria, after every conniving thing she did to me she always ended it with a wink.

I shake those thoughts away, not realizing that I literally shook too.

"Uhh, you good?" Steph asks me with a confused face.

"Oh yeah, just ignore me," I say turning my back to make Steph a cup of coffee.

"Yeah that's probably best," she looks at me like I've gone mental, which I have.

"Have you talked to Mia? How was her date?" I ask intrigued.

"She said it was good! They're going out again this weekend!" Steph says excited on Mia's behalf.

"Good for her," I say meaning it.

I finish with Steph's coffee and cautiously slide it her way. We drink our morning coffee together, with last night's tension completely evaporated.

When I'm all finished getting ready, I grab my purse and phone on my way out.

The drive seems way too short this morning as I anxiously pull into the parking lot. I walk in, greeting the receptionist as I now know as Natalie. I take my nervous steps to Nick's or I guess my new office.

Nick is on the phone half sitting on the desk and half standing with one leg on the ground looking fine as ever in a dark gray short-sleeved shirt and blue jeans.

Pretty sure I just missed a breath.

He holds up his index finger indicating he'll just be a minute.

He hangs up with whoever he was talking to about an upcoming project from what I've gathered.

He looks me up and down, "missed the memo? It's casual Friday," he chuckles.

I look down at myself, I'm wearing a black pencil skirt and a beige sleeveless blouse. I shrug my shoulders, "guess so."

"Alright, well let's get to it," Nick says standing up off the desk and sitting in the chair behind the desk.

I sit next to him in my usual spot.

"I like what you did with the place," he says looking around.

"Thanks," I say with a smile.

"So where do you want to go tomorrow night?" He asks the dreaded question.

I shrug my shoulders, "I don't know, something casual?" I ask, not wanting anything romantic.

"Okay sure, I'll think of something." He says.

"Okay," I say shyly and he smiles at my loss of confidence.

The rest of the work day is spent with me being way too shy, Nick packs some of his belongings because come Monday he's transferring to the Santa Barbara location.

It'll either suck if the date goes well or be a blessing if it doesn't and I still don't know which way I want it to go.

X hovers my mind throughout the day and I try to get it to subside but it's just not working. I catch myself thinking about what he's doing now that we're over, has he moved on? Has he gone back to his old ways? The thought makes my stomach hurt, would he feel the same as I do if he knew that I've taken an interest in someone else?

Chapter 39

POV

Millie

Saturday morning.

Tonight is my date with Nick that I completely regret initiating.

It's just one date, if it goes south he'll be leaving in two days anyway. I'm so not ready for any of this, I haven't gone on a real date with someone in a while and it's nerve-wracking.

I sit at the table in the suite drinking my morning coffee, not black, but with plenty of French vanilla creamer when Steph comes strolling out of the room like a hot mess with her hair everywhere and yesterday's makeup in all the wrong places. She wasn't home when I got home yesterday but I heard her stroll in late last night.

"Tonight's the night huh?" She asks in a sleepy voice.

"Yeah...do you think you can call me in sick for it?" I ask humorously.

"No baby girl, you did this to yourself, now you gotta follow through, no saving you tonight." She says through a yawn and tapping the top of my head.

"So where were you all last night?" I ask her.

She grins widely.

"At my new place.." she says with a smile that's revealing too many teeth.

I cock my head to the side, "what do you mean...?" I ask genuinely confused.

"Eee! Julian asked me to move in with him!" She says ecstatically.

"Oh my god, no way! Steph are you kidding me? I'm so happy for you!" I say wholeheartedly happy for her.

"And to think a few weeks ago you didn't even want to look him in the eye," I say rolling my eyes.

"I know! It's crazy isn't it?!" She asks waking up more.

"I'm so happy right now, give me that coffee I need it more than you, I gotta get ready to go home," she says snatching away my coffee and dancing around with it as if it's Julian.

I laugh at her silliness and am grateful for her shift in emotions from the other night.

I genuinely am so happy for her and Julian.

After about an hour, Steph leaves to go to her new home and I hop in the shower overthinking everything about this past week. I still feel completely heartbroken but every day is becoming a little less excruciating than the last.

It'll be good for me to get out regardless of whether it's a date or not, I need to be around more people and just let loose.

I watch a new YouTube tutorial on beachy appearing waves for my hair and by the grace of god I execute it. I apply a shimmery brown eyeshadow, add an extra layer of mascara than usual, and swipe on a glossy layer of lipgloss with a touch of shimmer.

I have no idea where we're going tonight but we agreed on casual so I pull out a pair of light-washed jeans that have a rip on the knee with a little kick at the bottom. I decide on a white off-the-shoulder top with ruched crisscrosses throughout. The fit is snug in all the right places and I'm finally gaining some confidence back.

I look through my bag digging through to find a gold necklace and bracelet and feel the familiar fabric of X's hoodie that I shoved at the bottom of my bag days ago. I shouldn't pull it out but I do.

I hold onto it in my arms and it still smells like him.

The scent I'll just never forget.

I contemplate going on this date with Nick more than ever before as I hold the hoodie close to me.

I'm too late though, my phone dings, it's Nick letting me know he's out front.

Here goes..

Chapter 40

POV

Millie

I step outside of the hotel and right in front is what I'm assuming is Nick's gray car.

He rolls down the window, "hey em," he says with a smile and my nerves are in overdrive.

I get in and we lightly converse about our days as we drive for what seems to be only about five minutes when we pull into a restaurant, Blue Lagoon the sign on the building reads.

We step out of the car and I'm thankful when we walk in and the atmosphere seems casual. There are sharks and other sea life creatures hanging on the walls. A hostess greets us and then guides us to a table alongside a window that has a view of the ocean. The sun is starting to set giving the sky an orangey hue. The scene brings me back to all of the nights spent with X and the deep conversation we've had that made us fall in love in the first place. Sitting here with Nick is feeling off-kilter but I need to make new memories even if it hurts in the process.

A waitress walks over to our table introducing herself as Ashley. She pours water into the glasses in front of us.

We order some cocktails as we glance over the menu. I have my head down deciding on what I want to order when I hear Nick say, "Penny?"

I glance up from my menu and I swear my eyes practically bulge out of the sockets.

Penelope?!

My whole body is frozen at the sight of her and on top of it Nick knows her?

"Em, this is Penny, we used to work together, what like 4 years ago?" He asks her as he looks her up and down, clear as day checking her out.

What surprises me more than my date checking out another woman, is the fact that it's not bothering me like it should.

"Yeah, something like that," Penelope says to him.

This is a real nightmare, the last time I saw this whore was a week ago, and naked at that. Wow, the balls this girl has to come up to us right now is literally mind-blowing.

"So what are you doing here Penny? What have you been up to?" Nick asks her.

You've got to be kidding me right now...

"I just started bartending here, I just wanted to say hi to you guys, maybe we can talk later Millie?" She asks looks down at me and I just want to throw my water at her overly made-up face.

"Mmm," I say with a fake smile.

"Okay, well I'll leave you guys to it," she says before walking back behind the bar as Nick stares at her ass the whole time.

I clear my throat to indicate that I noticed.

"Sorry, um how do you know Penny?" He asks me in confusion.

"Oh, uh, it's a long boring story, let's save that for another time," I say wanting to avoid the topic at all costs.

What the hell can she even want to talk to me about? And since when am I Millie to her? I've always been Nellie.

This date is in turmoil before it's really even begun, first the ocean view, then Penelope, and then my date checking Penelope out what else can possibly happen tonight?

Ashley sets down our cocktails in front of us and I take a nice long sip needing it faster than it's going down. Nick excuses himself to use the bathroom and as soon as he does Penelope doesn't waste a minute taking his spot.

"What is it, Penelope?" I ask downing my drink and not wanting to say a single thing to her, I'd rather just talk with my fists but we're in public so I have to appear civil.

"I'm sorry Millie. I just got in over my head being at that house, I wanted to be like them and just be near them all the time and I don't know...I just was really shitty to you and I wanted to apologize even though I know it doesn't mean anything to you." She says and I think her apology may be sincere but what happened can't be taken back.

I just want her to leave so I say, "apology accepted."

She gives me a half smile, "Nick's a really good guy."

I don't know if she's telling me that or herself at this point and I don't give a shit either way.

She stands up from the chair, "I'm sorry to hear about what happened to X," she says gently and with a sad expression.

Hold the fuck up.

She starts to step away but I grab her wrist preventing her from doing so.

"What happened to X?" I demand and her face goes blank clearly unaware of me not knowing something she does.

"Oh..um nothing, nothing. I should get back to the bar," she says nervously trying to escape.

I stand up, pushing her against the wall to corner her with my arms on either side of her.

"What the fuck happened to X?" I say in a harsh tone.

She looks down awkwardly.

"Uhh, I'm sorry I just thought you would've known.." she says with furrowed eyebrows.

"Penelope, so help me god, if you don't start getting actual words out of that mouth of yours I will deck you right in your fucking plastic face in front of this whole restaurant with a smile on my psychotic face." I threaten.

She knows I'm not messing around, she looks me straight in the eyes and delivers excruciating news.

"He um..he overdosed the other day.." she says glumly.

No.

No. No. No

"When?" I ask panicked.

"Wednesday night." She says quietly.

"No" I whisper.

"I'm so sorry Millie, I thought you knew," she says embarrassed.

"No, I didn't fucking know," I say half enraged, half hurt that no one told me.

It all makes sense now, Steph knew. That's why she's been acting all weird since then.

What the fuck!

I don't even know my emotions right now, I'm feeling every single one of them all at the same time.

X overdosed?

How could he? How could he do this?

My heart rate is accelerating to the point that I feel the blood pumping in my ears, I need to get to him. I need to see him, I need answers.

I remove my hands from the sides of Penelope.

"I need your car," I demand.

"What?" She asks full of confusion.

"I need your car Penelope, if you want my forgiveness then give me your car for one night." I say desperately.

She gives in, pulling keys out of her denim shorts and hands them to me.

"What about Nick?" She asks.

"Penelope, I have bigger issues to deal with right now," I say matter of fact.

"Well, what should I tell him when he comes back?" She asks looking at the table.

"I do not give a fuck what you say," I tell her as I leave as fast as I can.

X.

X is my only priority right now.

Chapter 41

Millie

I'm briskly walking around the parking lot trying to locate Penelope's car, pressing the panic button, I'm not sure what is panicking more, me or the red Ford Fusion a few rows away.

This girl and red I swear..

Never mind that, I need to get to X.

It takes me way too long to get there, a place I never wanted to return to ever again in my existence can't come into view soon enough.

I have no nerves, I just need answers and I need them now.

I pull up onto Sunset Avenue and drive a hundred feet until the house comes into view.

I type in the gate's passcode as fast as my fingers can manage and it takes an eternity for the tall black wrought iron to open, once it finally does, I speed to any parking spot available.

I run out of the car as fast as I can and run into the front door, getting looks from some of the nearly naked girls sitting around with drinks in hand.

It's Saturday night so he could be at the club, god I hope he's not there and with some girl on top of him. My first instinct is to go to the penthouse so I run to the elevator pressing the button as it lights up.

"Come on, come on!" I say quietly to myself.

Honestly, I have no idea why I'm in such a rush, this happened days ago but I need the information.

The shiny stainless steel elevator doors separate and I step in immediately, pressing the button that reads four.

I impatiently stand there waiting for the elevator to reach my destination.

I have an overwhelming feeling of all the shit that went down here only a week ago and had this been a half hour ago, before I found out about X I'd be in a current state of panic by my surroundings but it's not thirty minutes ago, it's now and I need to get to him more than ever before. I feel responsible for this, deep down I know it was his decision but on the surface, he did this because of me.

The doors open and I'm on the fourth floor, anxiety is starting to take over after every step I take getting closer to X's black door.

I take a deep breath in and a deeper exhale out and knock on that door with so much force it inflicts pain on my knuckles.

Julian opens the door.

"Where is he?" I demand.

"Millie, it's not a good idea," he says rubbing the back of his neck.

"And it was a good idea to withhold his overdose from me?!" I ask enraged.

He lets out a loud exhale, "Who told you?"

"What does it even matter Julian?" I ask pushing him out of the way to let myself in.

Oh hell no!

"Are you fucking kidding me, Stephanie?" I say feeling fully betrayed as my best friend sits on the black leather couch.

"Millie, please don't be mad, I wanted to tell you about it but I didn't think you could handle the news yet," she says.

"That's not for you to decide Stephanie," I say pissed off.

She puts her head down with guilt, "I was just trying to protect you," she says with sadness.

"We'll talk about this later, where is he?" I more or less demand than ask.

"He's in his room," Steph says pointing to the hall.

I storm down the hall and when I reach the room I spent many nights in, I don't bother knocking I just open the door.

What the fuck happened in here?

It's a complete disaster in the room, lamps are lying on the floor, glass lies throughout the ground, and paper is ripped on the ground.

It's my note to him, he ripped up my note?

He's not in the bedroom but I see a glimmer of yellow and orange on the balcony, the fire pit is going.

I carefully step over the glass to avoid getting any in my shoes, I slide open the door that leads to the balcony and there he is.

He's sitting alone in a chair watching the fire in front of him, he's wearing his black hoodie with the hood above his head and in black basketball shorts with his legs crossed at the ankle with a joint between his fingers.

"X," I say sternly.

Fuck me, he meets my eyes in the sexiest way and then breaks contact giving his attention back to the flames and not giving me the time of day.

"Let's go to the beach, let's talk" I suggest.

"No," he says cooly.

"X, you owe me an explanation," I say crossing my arms over my chest.

"I don't owe you shit," he says calmly but feels like a stab to my heart.

"What..?" I ask simmering down my tone.

"Go away Millie, I don't want you here," he says with another stab to my heart causing me to actually lose a breath.

"I thought.." I start to say but he cuts me off still not looking my way.

"Whatever you thought Millie was wrong, now just leave," he says and I'm now holding back painful tears with his words.

What changed? A few days ago he was at the hotel door wanting me back and saying I love you and now? Now he couldn't be any more frigid towards me.

I rub my arms to comfort myself.

"No, I'm not leaving, what changed?" I ask losing all confidence.

"Shouldn't you be on a date right now? What are you still doing here?" He spits out.

Great..he found out..

"So that's what this is about?" I ask.

"Fuck you, Millie, I'm done with this conversation." He says full of hate.

"Don't talk to me like that, you're the one that messed up, not me," I say still lacking confidence because of my state of distress.

He shakes his head, once again not looking at me, and says, "Ya know, I know I fucked up. But you see the difference here Emily is that what I did was nothing more than just trying to get a deal out of it, was it wrong? Fuck yeah but I didn't have any feelings for her, she was nothing to me. But you? You caught feelings for someone, not even a week after all this shit went down, so go back to your date, he's probably waiting for you to put out unless you already have." He says emotionless like the fucking devil.

I walk over in front of him and slap him so hard across the face.

"Fuck you, you fucking pathetic hypocrite," I say fully enraged.

He sits there like I didn't just make his face red from my hand and didn't just spit hateful words his way.

"Get your sorry ass up off this chair and get your ass down to the beach, now! You do owe me an explanation and I'm not leaving here until I get!" I say gaining all of my confidence back.

He looks up at me with his hands in surrender, "Okay Jesus.."

Chapter 42

Damn, this woman is fucking abusive lately.

The faster we have our little pointless talk on the beach the faster she'll leave.

I can't even look at her, she looks fucking beautiful right now, but it's not for me it's for whoever she transferred feelings for.

I keep my head down following her out of the bedroom where I let all my frustrations out the other night.

We walk through the living room where Steph is crying and Julian is consoling her, I hate them right now. They're moving in together and here I am alone as always and always will be.

Millie ignores the couple on the couch, as do I as I follow her out of the penthouse.

We take the stairs rather than the elevator and If I just play by the rules it'll all be over fast enough.

We make it outside and I can smell the smoke from my balcony from out here. Luckily I didn't lose my joint, after I stood up from my comfortable spot on my chair, I placed the joint behind my ear. I'm gonna need this shit before, during and after this lecture.

We walk through the beach as Millie is still leading the way and my shoes are collecting sand as we go.

We reach the shoreline and she sits herself cross-legged.

"Sit down." She demands.

"I don't want to," I say rebelling against her.

"Sit the fuck down," she says not taking no for an answer.

My god she's so feisty lately.

I sit down with my feet planted on the sand and my knees bent with my hands supporting me from behind.

"Talk." She says wasting no time.

"What do you want to know?" I ask annoyed.

"Everything." She simply states.

"Yeah well, I don't know what to tell you," I say wanting this to be over so I can just be in peace with my best friend Mary Jane.

"Okay, fine. 20 questions, we'll both ask each other hard questions and we can't turn it down, no one wins, no one loses." She proposes.

"Ughh," I say with a dramatic exhale not wanting to play this stupid fucking game but I want this to be over and it won't be until she gets her way.

"Fine, go," I say agitated.

"Why did you do it, I know you're a huge drug dealer, you know better, so why did you do it?" She asks.

"Because I wanted an escape. I went too far and I didn't mean to." I explain.

"Your turn," she says to me looking my way but I don't look at her, I can't.

"Do you like this guy?" I ask really wanting to know.

"I don't know, honest answer, in ways yes and in ways no." She says and it hurts like a bitch.

"What happened when you overdosed?" She asks straight forward.

I shrug my shoulders, "I went unconscious, threw up, got confused, called our medic Millie, lost consciousness again, seized, died for a minute, and then woke up trying to call out for you." I explain and look over to her as I say the last words. She's crying and I want to hug her and assure her I'm fine but my pride gets in the way of that.

"Why did you go out with him?" I ask trying to change the subject.

"Because I was mad at you, I wanted to get you back for what you did to me." She says and it makes me feel like shit for giving her such a hard time about it.

"What did it feel like to die?" She asks quietly and slowly.

"It felt good, it felt amazing actually," I say with honesty in my words.

She nods her head.

"Millie, your parents are at peace," I say fully looking at the shattered woman in front of me.

She nods her head again.

"Are you going to go on a second date with this guy? Have you kissed him or anything else?" I ask starting to get heated by the thought.

"That was two questions, but no to both of them." She says quietly.

"What really made you want to mix the alcohol and pills?" She asks and I'm about to hurt her with my answer.

"You and my mom," I say regretfully.

She depressively nods her head again.

"I'm sorry." She says sobbing and covering her hands with her face. I finally have the courage to hug her for comfort and the feeling of her in my arms brings me back to the place where I felt complete peace and serenity.

"It's not your fault baby, it's mine, I'm sorry I did this to you," I say wiping away a tear from her cheek.

"Millie, I promise you, I'll never do it again," I say wiping away another tear.

"I was stupid, and I was desperate to stop my hurt," I say brushing the hair away from her face.

"Why does everyone I get close to have to die, or almost die? Why does this happen to me?" She says sobbing.

"Mil, listen to me, you are not responsible for the actions of others, you're just the unfortunate one to be caught in the middle," I say emphatically.

"Can I say something harsh?" I ask hesitantly.

"Since when do you ask?" She says.

"Okay, you got me there," I say.

"Go on," she says waiting for me to speak my harsh words.

"I understand why your dad did what he did, Millie," I say and she looks confused.

"Your dad, he didn't turn to drugs to hurt you, he did it because he felt he couldn't live another day without your mom and I can relate to that. I felt as though I couldn't live another second without you, I dove into the pills and alcohol because I was desperate to feel numb. It was so wrong of me Millie, it was cowardly of me because I didn't deserve the numbness, I deserve the pain for what I did." I explain to her.

"What was so harsh about that?" She asks.

"Your dad was a coward, Millie, he took the easy way out more than once to mask the pain and dragged you down with him. He was a selfish man that couldn't be strong enough for you. I may be like your father in this instance but the difference here is that your dad had something to still live for, I had nothing, it's like, I don't know, what's the point of being alive if you're not really live?" I say truthfully.

She looks up at me, "so I'm nothing? I'm not worth the effort? I'm not something to live for?" She asks breaking my heart.

"Millie, that couldn't be further from the truth, you are everything," I say honestly, and what she does next shocks the hell out of me.

Chapter 43

POV

Millie

I don't know why I do it but I push his hug away and straddle him. He's clearly surprised by my shift in behavior.

He looks up at me, and although it's dark out now, the reflection of the moon and polluted Los Angeles sky glistens on his green eyes.

He's searching my face trying to figure out what's going on in my mind, I spare him the thoughts and take both of my hands on either side of his face and bring my lips to his.

He accepts them with ease, our kiss starts off with closed lips and continues on with our tongues entangled, making up for lost time.

This is the happiest I've felt all week and even though I can't actually read his mind, I know the same is true for him.

He pulls me in closer wrapping an arm around my waist and the other still behind him supporting us. He breaks from the kiss only for a second, "fuck baby, I miss these lips," he says so seductively.

"I've missed yours," I say bringing my lips back to his full soft ones.

He sits us forward, taking both hands on either side of my waist, and flips us over so I'm lying underneath him.

The lust in his eyes are intense before he moves his lips to my neck causing me to shiver at the sensation.

He sucks and gently nips at my neck sending me into sexual overdrive.

The hardness I feel pushing into my leg snaps me out of the lust-filled moment we were just in.

The thought of him pushing that same dick into someone else only one week ago overtakes my mind.

X notices my shift and breaks away from our kiss. He doesn't say anything, just sits up, running his fingers through his hair.

"Sorry," he says breathlessly.

I glance at him, "I was the one that came on to you remember?"

He shrugs a shoulder.

"I should probably get going," I say looking out to the ocean.

"Yeah, okay." He says with a raspy voice.

We walk back together off of the beach and our eyes are set on the beautiful fountain. Neither one of us says a word we just bring our feet there.

The beautiful sound of the water continuously flowing from tier to tier is so calming.

I take a penny out of my purse and close my eyes thinking of a wish and then throwing it in.

X laughs and it's a sound I've missed.

"What are you doing?" He asks.

"Making a wish.." I say in an obvious tone.

He chuckles, "Got another penny?" He asks and ew that word penny brings me back to the awful date that only occurred an hour ago.

I push away the thoughts of it all, I want to just enjoy the sliver of happiness for a little while longer. I reach into my purse pulling out another penny and hand it to him.

He closes his eyes, requesting a wish in his head, and then throws it into the water.

He looks over to me, "What'd you wish for?" He asks.

"I can't tell you, it won't come true then," I say so matter of fact.

He chuckles, "Did you ever get that pony?"

I roll my eyes, "touché."

"What did you wish for?" I ask him wanting to know first.

"You," he says so simply and my heart accelerates.

"I wished that I could forgive you," I say quietly.

"Well, I hope both of our wishes can come true one day." He says with meaning behind the words.

"Me too," I say watching the water fall.

"Okay well, I should probably go now," I say breaking the moment we're having.

"Okay, goodnight Millie." He says softly and turns his back walking away.

The words escape me without thought, "So where are we meeting tomorrow?" I ask after him.

He stops at the words spoken, only turning his head with a slight smile, "same place?"

And we both go our separate ways for the night.

Chapter 44

POV

X

This was not how I was expecting this night to go in any way.

Wasn't expecting to see Millie, wasn't expecting to have a heart to heart and sure as fuck wasn't expecting her to kiss me.

Fuck that kiss was hot. Of course I had to be a dumbass and take it too far but I just couldn't help myself at the time.

I haven't had any sexual encounters in a week which is a long ass time for me, unfortunately my last sexual experience was with the wrong person or I guess people...

I walk back into the house, making my way up to my place and smiling to myself like a little girl but I don't care how stupid I look, she wants to see me tomorrow, she used my words I used on her when we first met.

Man, I love this girl.

I can tell she's trying to forgive me, she's fighting within herself for me but she's losing the battle and I couldn't be an happier. We have a long way to go until we can go back to where we once were but I'm okay with that, I'm okay with taking baby steps even if it takes the rest of our lives to achieve that.

This woman is worth the wait, I don't want anyone else, I only want her and I don't think that'll ever change, she's a once in a lifetime sort of love.

I unlock my door with the keycard, Julian and Stephanie aren't here anymore, thank fuck. They've been so overbearing since the whole incident it's like having parents around again.

I dodge the glass on my bedroom floor and walk out to the balcony, sitting in my previous spot. I watch the fire in complete bliss this time around. The fire in front of me is matching the fire within in, in the best way possible. I actually have a chance with Millie again, just an hour ago I was hopeless, and now I am hopeful.

After another fifteen minutes of watching the flames in the pit roar, I put out the fire and go back inside.

I lay myself on the bed feeling the best I've felt in days, I should probably clean up the disaster in here but right now I just want to lay here in bliss with the woman I love flooding my mind.

I haven't gotten off in so long and probably won't for as equally long. I'm a man that gets pleased whenever I want but Millie is the only one I want for that job, so waiting it is.

God didn't provide me a hand for no reason, I pull down my shorts and glide my hand up and around the head causing the sensation to make me breathless.

I think about Millie with every stroke. How fucking hot she was tonight with her feisty attitude, I think about the times we fucked and how even though she hasn't fucked around by a fraction of what I have, she fucks like a pro. Oh god and the taste of her, that taste, I'm craving it.

I stroke myself continuously, overtaken by just the thoughts in my own mind until I come undone, because of her.

When I get out of the much needed shower, I pull on new boxers and climb into bed. I'd do anything just to have her in bed with me again, not for sex but just to lay with him in my arms.

I'm bothered that Millie went on a date tonight, but she told me it was just to get me back, which I deserved and then some. As long as she never looks his direction again and vise versa , I'll let him keep his life.

I need everyone out of our business and out of our way if we're going to salvage this relationship.

Soon enough, one day at a time, I'll get my girl back, I can just feel it in my bones.

Chapter 45

POV

Millie

I'm driving back to the hotel in Penelope's car with thoughts of X taking over my mind in every way until they whither away with other thoughts from the night.

Tonight was unexpected, I feel slightly guilty for blowing off Nick in the middle of our date but he was no saint at the same time.

And Penelope? She works as a bartender now? That's all due to the shit that went down a week ago. I'm stunned she apologized for her actions towards me but it's Penelope..

I pull into the parking lot having no idea how I'll get this car back to Penelope, but right now I don't care either.

As I'm walking into the hotel lobby, I see Nick sitting on a couch, what is he doing here?

"Nick?" I ask out to him.

"Em," he says standing up off of the couch.

"What are you doing here?" I ask confused.

"I came here to see why you left, what happened?" He asks curiously.

"A lot?" I more or less say than ask.

"Care to share?" He asks while looking me dead in the eye.

I scratch the back of my neck, "do you want to come up to my room and we'll talk?" I ask.

"Okay," he says.

We take the elevator up to the third floor together in awkward silence. We reach the door and I unlock it, letting us in. Thank god Steph isn't here. I pull out a bottle of wine, pouring us each a glass, knowing that I'll need it for whatever conversation we're about to have.

"So?" he asks as I hand him the glass of wine.

"I'm sorry I left, there was something important I had to deal with and honestly Nick, I didn't like how you were checking Penelope out, what did you expect me to do?" I say chugging down the wine.

"Em, I wasn't checking her out, not in that way at least. I used to work with Penny, like years ago and she looked a hell of a lot different back then, I kind of couldn't stop looking at all the work she's had done." Nick explains and I just don't know him well enough to buy it or not.

I'll give him the benefit of the doubt for now.

"Okay," I say into my glass taking a sip.

"You know, the night is still young, how about a do-over?" He asks with hope written all over his face.

Oh god, what am I supposed to say? He's standing right in front of me and if I say no it'll be so uncomfortable.

"What did you have in mind?" I regretfully ask.

"Maybe just a walk?" He suggests.

Okay, I can do that, it's simply just taking step after step, no tension, no pressure, just a walk with some conversation.

"That sounds perfect to me," I say because it does.

We put our glasses down on the counter and head out the door for our walk.

Once we make it outside, we walk through the parking lot and find the sidewalk to start our do-over date, walking side by side.

"So, uh, how is Penelope getting home? I kinda figured you'd be giving her a ride..and to be honest I kinda thought she'd be giving you one too." I say nonchalantly.

"What? Seriously Em? How much of a piece of shit do you think I am?" He asks offended.

"Well.." I start to say but he stops me in my tracks.

"Em, I promise you, I'm not into her, like at all." He says trying to reassure me.

I nod my head and we start to walk again, the night is a beautiful warm one with a light breeze, it's a Saturday night so there are people out and about going in and out of restaurants and other establishments on the strip we're waking on.

"So who's the guy you had to see?" He asks and I wish he didn't. I'm not sure how to answer his question, because it's a question I don't know the answer to myself.

"He's uh, I don't know, I don't know how to describe him exactly," I say awkwardly.

"An ex?" He asks.

"If you can even call it that. We were never technically in a relationship and I caught him in a foursome, one of them being Penelope.." I say giving away more information than I initially intended to.

"Woah, woah, woah! What?!" He asks stopping his steps.

"Yeah.." I say scratching my hairline.

"Em, what the fuck?" He says in complete shock.

"And penny? Seriously? Wow...Em, I'm so sorry," he says genuinely. I shrug my shoulders.

"So why in the world did you have to see him, I mean it's fine, but why?" He asks still not moving from his previous halted steps.

"He uh," I start to say but I don't want to give away X's private issues.

"It's okay Em, I don't need to know," he says sensing my hesitation and I couldn't be more grateful that he's not pressing it.

Although I told X not long ago that going on a date with Nick was to get back at him, I don't know if that holds the truth so much anymore. Nick is easy, he doesn't come with a ton of baggage like X does and he seems to be more the understanding type, not to mention he's almost as handsome as X too. This would kill X if he knew that my feelings for Nick had gone back on track.

As if my mind can be read, I hear my phone ding in my pocket, I pull it out, it's a text from X,

Can't wait for tomorrow, baby

But I don't reply.

After another fifteen minutes of walking around and keeping the conversation lighter than the previous one, we reach the front of the hotel.

"I'm glad we got a do-over, Em," Nick says.

"Yeah, me too," I say meaning it.

"Just know.." he's moving closer to me and suddenly planting his lips on my cheek.

"I'd never do what he did to you, anyone else would be a downgrade." He whispers in my ear.

For the second time tonight, I surprise myself by taking his face into my hands and connecting my lips to his.

Chapter 46

POV

X

I texted Millie but she must be sleeping by now.

I want to make tomorrow special, we've never been on a real date before so I want to make the beach into a date setting.

My mind is filling with ideas of what to do for her, how can I make this special for her? I've never actually been on a real date so I have no idea what I'm doing.

I know a few things that I want to do to make things as personal as they can be, but when it comes to the setup, I'm lost.

Who better to ask than her best friend?

I get out of bed and put some sweatpants on. I leave the penthouse and go down to the third floor walking to Julian's place.

I'm briskly walking down the hallway when..Oh great...

I keep my head down not wanting to make eye contact.

"So I just don't even exist anymore?" Adria asks.

"Told you not to talk to me," I say coldly keeping my head down.

"Heard Emily is having quite a night with some guy." She says snakily.

"Shut the fuck up, Adria," I say and walk past her not wanting to hear about it.

Word travels fast, but what isn't traveling fast enough, is that Millie ditched her date to come back to me so fuck everyone and whatever they think.

I reach Julian's door and bring my knuckles to the black door giving it a knock.

After a few minutes of impatiently knocking, Julian opens the door and without invitation, I let myself in.

"Where's Stephanie? I need her opinion on something." I say.

"Dude, where is your fucking shirt?" He asks me not answering my question so I won't answer his.

Stephanie comes out of Julian's bedroom dragging her hands through her blonde hair.

Oops...At least one of us is getting some.

"Stephanie, I need your help," I say not wasting any time.

"Is everything okay? What happened?" She asks worried.

"Yeah, yeah, everything is fine, actually everything is great," I say with a smile.

She looks surprised by my sudden change in attitude.

"Oh! Good. So what do you need help with?" She asks curiously.

"Millie and I are seeing each other tomorrow, I want to make it into a date, I want to do something special for her. Do you think you can help me?" I ask her.

"Wow, are you serious? So tonight went well then?" She asks with a smile.

"Yeah, it was rocky at first but it ended well," I say happily.

"Okay, well what are we waiting for? Let's get planning!" Stephanie says all giddy.

"Seriously man? We were kind of in the middle of something..." Julian says annoyed.

"Shut up man, just wait a few minutes, I haven't gotten any in a week, I just had to use my hand for the first time in like a year," I say equally annoyed.

"Oh my god dude what the fuck is wrong with you? My girl is right there and even if she wasn't, no one wants to hear that shit." Julian says running his fingers through his hair and leaving his hands on the top of his head.

"Just hurry up," he says.

Stephanie rolls her eyes at him, "C'mon X, let's get your girl back."

Yeah, let's get my girl back.

Chapter 47

Millie

As I walk back into the lobby alone this time, guilt washes over me. I couldn't help myself from kissing Nick. The spark in the kiss when our lips met didn't even come close to what X's did to me earlier but there still was something there.

I unlock my hotel room door that X has paid for and when I get in, I go straight to the bed to get my head in order. I love X and that is undeniable but what he did to me, was unforgivable, no matter how many pennies I throw into fountains trying to obtain that wish. And Nick.. oh Nick. He does not deserve this, he does not deserve half of my attention, half of my heart, half of me, while the other half belongs to someone else.

I feel awful for giving X the wrong impression tonight, I came on to him giving him false hope but he just has some sort of effect on me no matter what he does. When I'm with him I don't think straight, but when I'm with him I feel alive.

I look at my phone rereading the text he sent me an hour ago one too many times.

I text him back,

5 o'clock okay?

I can't lead him to believe we have a chance any more than I already have, tomorrow night, I need to have the hard talk with him, the we need to talk conversation.

...

Sunday morning, 5 more days until I get into my new apartment, I'm so close. I grab my phone and see two messages, one from Nick and one from X.

I open nicks first,

Thank you for last night, missing those lips already. I need to be back in L. A on Wednesday, can I see you?

That text makes my stomach do flip-flops in the best possible way. I text him back,

I'd love that

I now open the text from X dreading it,

Of course baby, I have a surprise for you

I don't reply to his message. God, what kind of surprise? Please don't make this harder on me than it needs to be.

...

It's now 3 o'clock and I've spent the day doing absolutely nothing but feeling nervous beyond belief for what needs to happen tonight. I've already showered and now I just need to do hair and makeup.

I do my hair in beachy waves, I add a light layer of lavender eyeshadow to my lids and apply a couple of coats of mascara to my lashes. It's a warm day so I pick out a lavender sun dress that is going great with the tan I've gained recently.

By the time I'm done getting ready, it's time to head to X's house to break his heart more than it already is.

I pull into the driveway feeling overwhelmed with anxiety, I notice the grand fountain first, it's lit up red. I drive a little closer and oh my god there he is. Sitting on the steps of the staircase with his legs slightly opened and his hands clasped together in between.

I park the car as fast as I can and get out.

"Woah.." I say in disbelief and he smiles brightly.

X is done the heck up. His hair is completely slicked back, showing every inch of his handsome face. He's wearing black fitted pants and a black fitted button-down shirt that is rolled up on his forearms showing off his tattoos. He looks so fucking incredible I can't get my breathing under control.

He slowly walks down the steps, taking a pair of sunglasses out of the pocket of his pants, he puts the sunglasses over his eyes and replaces the now-empty space in his pocket with his hands. I feel like I'm about to pass out at how goddamn attractive he is right now.

When he reaches me, he leans his head down and brings his lips to my ear, only a centimeter away. The scent of him is intoxicating and I'm in a high right now.

"You're making it obvious baby," he whispers into my ear and a smile breaks my lips apart at his words.

"You look beautiful too ya know," he says and he's pulling out all the old tricks on me.

I chuckle at his humor.

He takes my hand into his and guides me off the driveway and towards the beach.

I came here to officially break things off with him and the sight that sits in front of me has officially makes me halt at those thoughts.

Tears begin to gather in my eyes and I squeeze his hand within mine.

Chapter 48

POV

Millie

"X, what is all of this?" I ask looking up at him as he's looking down at me.

"Why don't you go see for yourself," he says leading me to the beautiful display.

As we get closer, more comes into view. Alongside the shore is a wooden pergola, dangling from the top are vintage Edison bulb lights giving off a beautiful glow. On each post of the pergola, are white orchids cascading over one another from top to bottom. On the inside sits a small fire pit with a fire roaring to life and two wicker chairs across from each other. It is the most beautiful thing I've ever seen and the most thoughtful that anyone has ever done for me. How much work went into this in such a short amount of time?

"X," I say trailing off not knowing what to say.

"C'mon baby, there's more inside," he says gently pulling my hand to see what more this could possibly entail.

We walk the rest of the distance and make it to the pergola. There's so much to see inside here. There is a black zip-up hoodie placed hanging on the back of the wicker chair and it makes me chuckle.

Delicately placed all over the sand on the inside, are things written on cocktail napkins that I can't quite read so I start picking them up one by one and reading them in my head.

I love you, I love your heart, I love your soul, I love your eyes, I love our connection, I love your beauty, I love our talks, I love your touch, I love your smile.

Napkin after napkin he has written reasons why he loves me. I don't even know what to think right now, this is unbelievable.

There is a small glass table off to the side with a bottle of wine and two glasses. An envelope lays on the top of the glass, I pick it up, "20 answers?" I ask him in confusion.

He chuckles with a wide handsome smile and I think I may fall to my knees at his appearance alone, "20 questions, but instead, it's just 20 answers, 20 things about me that I only want you to know." He says putting his hands in his pockets.

I flip over the envelope to open it but he stops me, "maybe just open it when you're alone, there's some embarrassing things in there," he says rocking back and forth on his heels.

"Okay," I say with a smile while nodding my head and setting it back down in its original location.

All of this, I look around some more, all of this is a representations of us.

"Some wine?" He asks breaking me of my thoughts.

"Um..yeah, thank you." I say quietly.

He walks over squeezing past me while placing his hand on my waist to keep me sturdy as he makes his way to the table next to me.

He's pouring wine into both glasses as I stand there continuing my thoughts. I came here tonight to break things off with him completely and somehow it made a one-eighty turn as it usually does when it comes to us.

He hands me a wine glass and our hands touch causing my fingers to feel electrified.

We sit across from one another watching the fire crackle from time to time, he reaches out from under his chair, pulling out graham crackers, marshmallows, and chocolate.

"S'mores?" I ask way too excitedly for my age.

He laughs, "fuck yeah baby."

He hands me the ingredients and we start to roast our marshmallows.

"Hey X?" I ask looking at him as he has his head down watching his marshmallow overcook.

He looks up, the glow of the fire is making his eyes greener and his nose ring shine, "yeah baby?" He asks.

"Um, thank you. Thank you for all of this." I say guiding my hand out to the surroundings of the pergola.

"Anything for you," he says staring into my eyes.

"Um, X? Your marshmallow is on fire.." I say pointing to the poor charred marshmallow succumbing to the flames.

"Oh shit!" He says waving it around causing the ball of fire to intensify and it oh so sadly drops into the fire.

I start laughing at the chaos that occurred just by trying to roast a marshmallow and he starts laughing too.

"Who taught you how to roast a marshmallow?" I ask through laughter.

"No one, this was my first time," he says honestly and it makes me sad that in his thirty-one years of life, he's never made a s'more.

"Here, have mine, and I'll make another, you and marshmallows don't mix," I say shaking my head and handing him over my marshmallow.

"Thanks, baby," he says taking it from me.

He assembles his s'more and takes a bite, "damn, this shit is good!" He says with a full mouth.

I laugh, "I know, why do you think I got so excited when you pulled them out?" I ask pointing to the s'more he's eating.

"Come here baby, have a bite since yours isn't done yet." He says extending the s'more to me.

I stand up and move over to the side taking a step towards him instead of leaning over the fire as he extends it straight in front of the fire somehow expecting me to take a bite through the flames.

I take a bite as he holds it out, he closely watches my mouth as if I'm doing something incredibly sexy and I swallow.

"You have a little something.." he says keeping eye contact with me as I look down at him. He takes his thumb to my bottom lip wiping away excess marshmallows. I take his thumb into my mouth sucking it away and his eyes become full of lust watching the show.

"Fuck.." he whispers.

With that, no initiation on either end, we both lean in for a kiss, the sweetness on our tongues colliding with one another.

Without breaking the kiss, X tosses the s'more into the fire. I break the kiss to look at the s'more engulfed in flames.

"That was a perfectly good s'more," I say disappointed.

"And these are perfectly good lips that require my full attention," he says while taking his hand behind my ear pulling my face to his direction, and connecting our lips again, deepening our kiss after every passing second as though it'll never be enough for us.

Chapter 49

POV

X

I can't get enough, her sweet lips on mine have taken me into euphoria.

Without removing her lips from mine, she straddles me the best she can given the small space on the wicker chair. I need to keep my cool, last night, I took it too far for what she was ready for and it scared her off. I let her take control only leaving my hands against her waist. She takes my hands guiding them from her waist to her ass. I miss this ass it's been way too long since I've had it in my palms.

I'm rock hard, just dying to push it up against her but I don't. I'm on unstable grounds here, she can pull away at any moment. I give her ass a good squeeze and she moans into my mouth giving me the verification that she's missed this just as much as I have.

She sits up on me breaking the kiss, leaving me desperate for more. Her lips are swollen in the sexiest way as I look up to her waiting for her next move.

"We should probably take it easy," she says looking into my eyes. I'm so disappointed by those words but we've gone a fuck of a lot further tonight than I ever expected so I guess I can't be too bothered by it.

She stands up, holding her hand out to me, "wanna go in the water?" She asks with a smile.

"What?" I ask chuckling.

"C'mon, I've yet to go into the ocean here," she says pleading with me to follow.

I shrug my shoulders, "fuck it," I say taking her hand and standing up too.

We walk closer to the shoreline hand in hand. She kicks off her shoes and puts her feet in and looks back to me encouraging me to follow.

I take off my socks and shoes, rolling up my expensive black pants that I just bought hours ago and put my feet in as well.

"What are you waiting for, aren't you gonna go in?" I ask the beautiful woman standing beside me.

She laughs, "No, I just meant go in as with my feet, I'm not submerging myself."

She's gonna fucking hate me but she already does so what the hell, I take my phone out of my pocket and toss it onto the shore. She's looking out at the ocean so I come up behind her taking her over my shoulder.

She yelps in shock, "What are you doing?!"

I walk us out more into the water, "we're going all in baby," I say meaning it literally and theoretically.

"No, no, no!" She yells out kicking her legs, "Have you never seen jaws?! This is how it starts! A huge shark is going to come attack us!"

I laugh and dunk us under the salty cold water.

"Oh my god!" Millie yells out wiping water from her face. "What is wrong with you?!"

"Don't know where to start and don't know where to end babe," I say honestly with a laugh.

She jumps on me trying to pull me under but is completely unsuccessful because of my size, I grab her body tossing her back into the water as the splash of her body soaks me more.

She re-emerges, "so unfair!" She says putting her hands on her hips.

"Woah! Did you see that?!" I ask putting on a frightened face.

"What?!" She says jumping onto me to save her and hugging me tightly for protection.

I start laughing, "I'm kidding baby."

She jumps off of me and pushes my chest hard causing me to fall into the water.

"Holy shit! How was the colder than the first time around?!" I ask as my clothes cling onto me for dear life.

"C'mon, let's get changed, you're shivering," I suggest.

We slowly walk towards the shore, making only small movements due to the density of the water.

We finally make it out and we're both freezing at this point, I run over to the pergola grabbing the black hoodie from the chair it's handing on, not actually thinking we'd need it. I run it, Millie, wrapping it arm her for warmth.

"Thank you," she says politely.

She grabs the napkins and the 20-answers envelope.

"Let's go upstairs," I say and she follows.

Chapter 50

POV

X

We walk up to the penthouse mostly in silence, dripping water from our bodies and onto the floor creating a trail until we reach my door.

When I get it opened, we walk inside taking small steps careful not to slip on the hardwood floors.

"I'll get us some towels," I say leaving Millie in the kitchen area.

I retrieve two white towels and wrap the white cotton around her first before drying myself off.

"C'mon let's get you some new clothes," I say walking down the hallway to my bedroom and she quietly follows behind.

I rummage through drawers finding sweatpants and a T-shirt, she'll drown in these clothes but I have no other options. I hand her my clothes and then rummage through again looking for clothes for myself.

"Thank you," she says quietly.

"Mhm," I hum out.

I take off my soaked button-down shirt and let it fall to the ground.

"I'll change in the bathroom, you can change in here, just let me know when you're done," I say walking to the bathroom.

I'm half in the bathroom, and half in the bedroom when she asks, "Um, hey X?"

I turn my head towards her, "yeah?" I ask.

"Do you think you can unzip my dress?" She asks and those words make me want to run over to her and not only unzip the dress but rip it off.

"Yeah, sure," I say instead.

I walk over actually feeling nervous, I need to contain myself and attempt to be a gentleman, something completely foreign to me, but when it comes to Millie, everything is foreign.

I stand behind her taking the small purple zipper between my thumb and middle finger, ever so slowly dragging the zipper down until it reaches the middle of her soft back.

She shocks the hell out of me, bringing my dick to life when she takes each side of the straps from her shoulders, to her arms and it lightly falls to the floor. She stands with her back to me, water delicately dripping from her hair and down her body. The image alone is enough to make me cum. She reaches behind her with both hands, unclasping her white bra and allowing it to drop to her feet.

I lean my head against her wet hair, just behind her ear, "what are you doing?" I whisper.

She doesn't say anything, she just cradles the back of my head with her left hand.

Green light.

I move her wet hair to the side, bringing my lips to her neck, gently sucking at the sensitive skin, she shivers either from the cold or my touch. I take both of my hands cupping her breasts, her nipples are so hard right now I just want them to occupy my mouth but I need to pace myself. She puts her hands over mine, encouraging me to continue on. I slowly trail my right hand from her right breast and move it to her stomach, letting the anticipation build for her. It feels as though all of the blood from my body has gone straight to my dick, I'm so hard right now, I just need to be in her but I don't think she'll let me. I tuck the tips of my fingers into the lacy fabric, the last article of clothing left on her. She's not halting my movement, so I bring my fingers closer to where they've been dying to feel for so long. The contact is finally made with my finger pad and her most sensitive spot. She leans her head against the space between my shoulder and neck, escaping a low moan of pleasure. I close my eyelids, getting myself into the same euphoria as her. My fingers are meticulously going to work as she loses herself around me. She turns around, grabbing just behind my ears and pulling me to her lips, these kisses alone are driving me into oblivion. She breaks away, releasing her hands from my neck, and takes my hand instead, guiding me to the bed.

We stand in front of each other just beside the bed and she takes the zipper of my wet pants between her fingers, dragging it down until it can't anymore. She takes the sides of my pants pulling them down as she goes down with it.

Is this actually fucking happening right now?

She pulls the sides of my boxers and takes them down my legs until I'm completely free of all clothing.

She takes me into her mouth, taking my dick in as far as her mouth will allow. I can't even help the way my head is falling back at the sensation.

"Fuck," I say and she tries to take me deeper.

I fist her hair in my hand, allowing my hand to follow her movements. I tilt her head back so she can look at me, "You're so fucking beautiful Millie." I say while she has a mouthful of my dick in her mouth.

"Get up baby," I gently demand.

She releases me and I already miss that wet, warm tongue of hers but I want a turn now.

"Lay down," I say delicately pushing her hips to lay down, when she does, I hover my body over hers.

I kiss her with meaning, lightly biting her bottom lip and sucking, causing it to swell. I move my lips to her neck, doing exactly the same as I did with her lips, and then move to her breasts, giving each one equal attention. She puts her palms on the top of my head and subtly pushes, indicating me to go lower.

I put a single finger on each side of her lace underwear peeling it away from her body.

Fuck, I need to get myself together. The image of her completely naked lying on my bed is driving me wild.

I give her exactly what she wants, trailing my tongue down, and giving faint nips until I reach where she wants my mouth the most. I barely bring the tip of my tongue over her swollen clit and she jerks. I put my hands over each of her forearms, holding them in place momentarily as I glide my tongue over her. She jerks again so I remove my hands, tucking my arms under her thighs and my hands on top of them, keeping her firmly in place.

"Breathe baby," I say before bringing my tongue back to her sensitive clit.

She tries to jerk again but my hands prevent her from doing so. After a few seconds, she calms herself down and enjoys what I'm giving to her. She runs her fingers through my damp hair and then tugging at the roots. This causes me to pick up the speed with my tongue, forcing moans from her. I remove one arm from her thigh and bringing my middle finger into her as I continue on with my tongue. She's becoming breathless, panting, she is so close. I remove my tongue, keeping my finger at work, I look up at her, "Come for me baby," I command.

Within seconds she's coming undone around my finger as she practically rips the strands of my hair from my head. It's so fucking sexy I can't even take it.

I put my mouth back to where it belongs, allowing my tongue to absorb the wetness of her release.

I'm apprehensive about the next step. Does she want me to continue on with the next part or will she deny me? I want her so fucking bad, I'm dying to be in her.

She saves me from my thoughts when she says, "I want you, X."

Chapter 51

POV

Millie

My entire mind and body have gone into overdrive. I missed his touch more than I originally anticipated. I don't know what made my mind change, was it the beautiful, carefree date? Or was it the image of him standing in the doorway with his shirt off and water dripping delicately from his body? I don't know either way and I don't care either way because right now, I want him more than ever. I want our bodies to become one.

X reaches over me, opening the bedside drawer. He fetches out a condom and kneels on the bed between my aching legs. He rips the top of the wrapper with his teeth and spits it off to the side.

"Are you sure about this baby? I don't want you to feel pressured." He asks looking down at me.

I don't say anything I just nod my head.

He slides the condom on, preparing for what's to come and the anticipation in me is building.

He slowly enters himself into me, I can't help the moan that escapes my lips.

"Fuck, I missed you." He says hoarsely.

He ever so slowly moves in and out of me, careful not to inflict any pain. He leans himself down bringing his mouth to my neck burying himself there.

He gradually picks up the pace with his thrusts and I don't know why my mind goes there but it does. I imagine X doing this to Aspen. I begin to feel all negative emotions, feeling the betrayal at its peak. I'm so humiliated when hot tears start falling down my face. I pray to god he doesn't notice.

"I love you, baby, I love you so much," he says through thrusts as tears continue their way down from my eyes collecting in one ear and the other side onto his cheek.

He notices.

He lifts his head up putting it directly in front of mine.

"Millie, what's wrong?" He asks fretfully.

"Nothing," I say wiping away my tears, "I'm fine."

"Baby, talk to me." He pleads.

"It's…" I can't get the words out because sobs take over instead. This is so embarrassing, I'm crying like a baby during sex.

He puts his forehead against mine, "It's too soon." He says taking my thoughts from my mind and out from his mouth.

"I'm sorry," I say through tears.

He pulls out of me, leaving me empty again.

"No baby, you have nothing to be sorry for, I'm the one that's sorry," he says brushing away a strand of hair from my face.

He removes his hovering body and lays beside me instead.

"What can I do to make this right?" He asks sounding defeated.

"I don't know, maybe just time," I say hoping that's the truth.

He takes my hand in his, kissing my knuckles, "I'll wait forever if that's what it takes," he says so sincerely.

I squeeze his hand in appreciation. This man can very clearly have anyone he wants at any given time. He could've just said fuck it and moved on to the life he once lived before he knew about my existence but he's not. He's trying really hard here to get me back and I'm now feeling guilty about it. I want to forgive him but I need the time to do so. I feel guilty for my interest in Nick but it's just so easy with him.

"I should probably go," I regretfully say.

"Please don't baby," X says desperately.

"I have to, I have work in the morning," I say.

"I can take you there tomorrow," he suggests in desperation.

"I don't have any of my things here X, I'm sorry," I say.

"Okay," he says giving up.

I stand up off the bed putting my bra and underwear back in their rightful place and put on the sweatpants and shirt on that X has loaned me.

X stands up doing the same. Once we're both dressed again in warm, dry clothes, he puts his hands in his pockets staring at me.

I walk over to him and kiss his cheek, "Thank you for tonight, it was beautiful."

"Anything for you Millie," he says again.

"I can walk you to your car," he suggests.

"No, no it's fine," I say and he looks as though he wants to fight me about it but decides not to.

"Okay," he says and embraces me in a long, tight hug. I never want him to let go.

He, unfortunately, releases me, I grab the napkins and the envelope.

"Goodbye X," I say softly.

"Goodbye, Millie." He says watching me leave.

I make my way down the elevator and onto the first floor, the thoughts of tonight fill my mind.

"When are you going to tell him?" I hear a voice from behind me.

Adria.

I turn around, "excuse me?" I ask.

She has her arms crossed with one hand balled into a fist under her chin with the bitchiest face on.

"I asked when are you going to tell him that you're seeing Nick?" She asks again as if I'm stupid.

"How do you even know about that?" I ask now crossing my arms too.

"Oh honey, how do I not know about it?" She asks in such a condescending manner.

Penelope, that little two-faced bitch. I knew I couldn't trust a damn thing she said.

"Well, Adria, it's really none of your business," I say matter of fact.

She laughs, "It's only a matter of time, Millie, you'll be nothing but an old memory to him and we'll be right back to where we were." She says living in her fantasy world.

I laugh back, "yeah, well I'm the one wearing his clothes right now," I say with a wink at the end.

I leave it at that and turn my back and walk away with her spitting out hateful words at me.

I can't help but laugh again once I get outside.

Delusional woman.

Chapter 52

POV

Millie

I drive myself back to the hotel, full of emotions.

I don't know how to feel about any of what happened tonight. I went there intending to break things off and then I have sex with him? What is wrong with me?!

When I get back to the hotel, I open the door and am shocked to see Steph sitting on the couch. I assumed she's been giving me space after last night's episode.

"Hey," I say faintly.

"Hey," she says at the same level of volume.

I set down the lavender sun dress and notes onto the kitchen counter and walk over to the couch sitting beside her. She looks me up and down confused by my clothing.

"Don't ask.." I say.

She gives me a shy smile.

"I'm sorry Mills, I was just trying to protect you," she says in despair.

"I know Steph, I know," I say understanding her point of view.

"Penelope told me.." I say with a loud exhale.

"What?!" She asks in shock.

"Yeah..small world, she bartends at the place Nick took me to," I say rolling my eyes.

"What the fuck..?" She states.

"Yeah, I almost had to beat it out of her," I say shrugging my shoulders.

She smiles widely, "Wish you would've."

"Me too," I say reciprocating the smile.

Especially now..

"Do you think you can forgive me?" She asks hopeful.

"Of course I can Steph, I love you," I say grabbing her to hug her.

I can never stay mad at her, she's my rock, she's more than my best friend, she's my sister.

"How did tonight go?" She asks with a smile.

How did she even know? She spares me the question, "I helped him," she says.

My eyebrows shoot up, "oh?"

"He came to our room last night asking for help, he wanted to plan a perfect date," Steph says.

"And how much of tonight did you do?" I ask curiously.

"He came up with all the ideas, I just helped execute it," she says.

"Well, it was lovely," I say.

I feel even more like shit now.

...

It's now Monday morning, my first day on my own. I drive to the office praying I've learned enough last week to lessen the struggle coming my way.

I greet Natalie and walk to my new office. I go through the morning with a breeze, luckily no hiccups yet. I hear my phone ding through my purse. It's Nick.

How's day 1 going?

Me: Good! Thanks for being a good teacher. How's day 1 in Santa Barbara?

Nick: It's going. Kinda wish I never transferred, didn't know there'd be a gorgeous girl in the office.

Oh, Jesus..

Me: Too bad, could've been fun

Nick: At least I'll get to see you Wednesday

Me: Any ideas of what we should do?

Nick: We could keep it simple and go for another walk. Maybe on the beach?

No, the beach is mine and X's thing

Me: How about just a pavement walk
Nick: Lol. You got it

...

I go the next two days with a breeze, I haven't talked to X since Sunday night and even though it sucks, he's respecting the time and space that I need. At the same time though, I'm disrespecting him by going out on another date with Nick tonight, which X doesn't know about. I don't like Nick the way I like X and honestly, I don't see it going all that far with us but I did tell him I'd see him again tonight so we'll see how that goes.

After work, I go back to the hotel that I'm only staying at for the next two days until I get into my new apartment. Since I showered this morning I just touch up my hair and make-up. I pick out a pair of dark denim shorts and a light blue long-sleeved shirt. I put on a delicate gold necklace with a matching bracelet. Nick should be here any minute so I sit on the couch scrolling through my phone until I get the text that he's downstairs.

I make it down within a few minutes, he's standing in the lobby looking as good as ever in jeans and a white T-shirt that is fitting him in all the right places.

"Ready to go?" He asks with a sexy smile.

"Absolutely," I say and he takes his hand in mine, kissing my knuckles the way X did only a few days ago.

At this point, I'm no better than X.

Chapter 53

POV

X

I haven't talked to Millie since Sunday night and it's killing me, I've picked up my phone countless times to call her but never went through with it. I want her to approach me when she's ready. I've been burying myself in work, if I take another phone call I think I'll just lose my shit.

Since I haven't been traveling since the whole incident, I've been doing extra work in the meantime. Making a deal with Hugo would've brought in so much money but honestly how much money do I really need? I have enough money to get me through two lifetimes. At the end of the day, the deal with Colombia was just to emit more power to myself.

I hear a knock at my front door from the office I've been practically living in for days. Please be Millie..

I walk through the hallway half excited, half nervous for what she'll say. Please don't break my heart any further. I open the door but I am sadly mistaken when it's not Millie on the other side, it's Adria..

"You really just don't know when to quit do you, Adria?" I ask annoyed.

"Yeah, well, I've got something you'll want to see." She says matter of fact.

"I highly doubt that...besides I told you if there's something you want to relay to me, you go through Julian," I say getting angry.

"This isn't business-related, it's Emily Hill-related." She says and she's caught my attention.

"Yeah, I thought that might intrigue you," she says with a lifted eyebrow, squeezing her way past me and plopping a cardboard-like envelope on my kitchen table.

She takes a seat, making herself at home and it's infuriating me but I want to know what she has to show me, so I close the door and sit across from her at the kitchen table.

"I don't have all night Adria, get to it," I say even though I do have all night but I don't want her here longer than she needs to be.

She slides me the envelope and then crosses her arms over her chest expectantly.

I apprehensively turn over the envelope and rip open the top, nervous to see the contents inside. I reach in and take out multiple photos. I bring the photos in front of my face to get a closer look, and wow, I can't believe my own fucking eyes.

"Mhm, recognize the guy?" Adria breaks me of my concentration.

"Nico.." I say in disbelief.

"How did you get these?" I demand.

I look at the pictures again, Millie and Nico.. what the fucking fuck. They are holding hands outside of the hotel that I paid for.

"I hired a private investigator," she says simply, "Penelope told me she saw them on a date Saturday night."

"Yeah well, I already knew about that Adria, she ditched him for me, so these pictures are bullshit," I say full of rage.

"Oh, but they're not X, you see, these were taken tonight." She says with a sly smile.

That can't be true.

"No," I say shaking my head.

"Yes," she says nodding hers.

"She's not the little saint you think she is X," she says getting under my fucking skin word after word.

"What are the fucking chances?" I ask mostly to myself looking back at the photos.

Adria is right, in these photos, she's wearing different clothes.

She picks up a picture which is now spread out on the table in front of us. "Aw look at this one X, they're kissing," she says as if I'm not in love with the woman in these photos.

I give her a death stare.

"What? Don't kill the messenger.." she fearlessly says shrugging her shoulders.

"Nico.." I say again in absolute disbelief as I stare at the prick. Why do they have to look so fucking happy? She should be miserable right now.

"Apparently he goes by Nick now." She says pointing to Nico in one of the pictures.

Nico...he used to work for me. He lived here for two years while he was putting himself through college. He was uneventful, listened to what I told him to do, which was my dirty work, and mostly kept to himself. If I'm being honest with myself he was a good worker and a decent person compared to the rest of us.

The fact that he was decent doesn't change the vile feelings I have towards him right now. Right now, he's out with my girl. This motherfucker is going to pay if he knew about Millie and me and still pursued her. What makes me even more livid is that he's probably just the right kind of person for Millie.

"Nick?" I ask myself out loud.

"Yeah, apparently they work together. They were seen together late Saturday night and then again tonight." She explains.

"Late Saturday night?" I ask thinking back to Saturday night. Did she see him again after seeing me? What the fuck?

I'm really starting to boil over now, they have another thing comin' tonight because I am about to wreak havoc on their little date. Enough is fucking enough with this little game of hers.

But first, there's something I need to do.

I stand up from the chair and stand behind Adria, I put my hands on her shoulders and she puts her tatted hands on top of my tatted hands.

"See X, all she's doing is breaking your heart, breaking up this house, breaking our deals, it's all because of her. You don't need that, we can go back to the way things were." She says so fucking delusional.

I lean my head forward with my face brushing up against her long black hair and I can feel her smile against my cheek.

I whisper into her ear, "You're right Adria, she did break a lot of things, but you? You just broke the contract."

Chapter 54

POV

X

"Did you even read the contract?" I ask laughing with my question.

I know the answer to that when she sits up straighter.

"No.." she says.

She makes it so damn easy for me.

"I did this for you, X!" Adria says panicked.

"No, Adria you did this for no one other than you," I say calmly, pressing my fingertips into her small framed shoulders and she flinches from underneath.

I'm about to show her who really is the boss in this house.

"But ya know, I am going to do something for me now, I haven't done anything selfish in a while and I owe it to myself to do this," I say whispering in her ear again.

"Please, X" she begs, she knows me well enough to know what's coming next.

"I wish I could say that this won't bring me any greater joy than what I'm about to do Adria, but it does. It didn't have to be this way, you could've just kept to yourself, did your job like everyone else but it just was never enough for you. I took pity on you when I allowed for you to stay but you know, deep down I knew you'd fuck up. I'm just surprised you fucked up this fast, what it's been like a week? I'm sorry Adria but everything in life has consequences. Because of your sneaky actions, I'm dealing with my consequences of not being with the woman I love. I'm sorry to say but it's now time for your consequences." I whispered into her ear again with eerie calmness, letting the fear in her mind build with every word.

"X..." she says as I allow that to be her last word.

I stand up straight again, closing my inner arm around her throat in a headlock, with every muscle in my body I use as much force as I can to snap her neck. The loud crack will probably forever haunt me, not because I just took Adria's life but because the sound was so gruesome. The weight of her head is resting on my arm, I release my arm from the heavy weight and her face falls straight down onto the kitchen table with force, another crack, her nose probably just broke.

I bend down again to the lifeless body, "a contract is a contract, Adria, you should've read it." I whisper into her ear and then pat her head, "You're so fucking stupid, you should've known better, it clearly stated if you broke the contract not only would you have gotten fired but it would also deem me whatever I consequence I sought necessary and Adria, this was so fucking necessary." I say and collect the photos from the table, putting them back in the envelope before the blood from her nostrils reaches them.

I take a step away to retrieve my phone from the office but look back waving the envelope in the air, "oh yeah, and thanks for these," I say and walk away.

I get my phone from off my desk and call my bodyguard, stone.

After a few rings he picks up, "what's up X?" He asks in his deep voice.

"I have a body I need you to dispose of," I say as if it's no big deal.

"Where?" He asks.

"The penthouse." I simply state.

"How much blood?" He asks.

"Minimal," I say.

"Okay, I'll be right there." He says and we hang up.

Within minutes Stone is knocking at the door. I let him in to do his this. He walks over to the kitchen looking at Adria's lifeless body.

"Is that..?" He asks pointing to Adria.

"Yeah, it's her," I say with no remorse.

"Took you long enough," he says shaking his head.

"Too long," I say

"Do your thing, man, there's something I need to do," I say and he nods his head.

With that, I leave the penthouse to go break up a date.

Chapter 55

Millie

As we're finishing up our two-hour-long walk, stopping plenty of times to sit and talk, we make it back to the hotel entrance.

"I had a really good time, Em," Nick says genuinely.

"Yeah, me too," I say with a smile.

"I still can't believe the way you jumped when you saw that mouse crawl out of that garbage bin," I say with a laugh.

"Hey! I was startled!" He says with a laugh.

"Yeah, yeah, whatever you say," I say teasing him.

"Well, I should probably get goin', you have an early morning," Nick says tilting back and forth on his heels.

"I mean...yeah...but we could maybe just have one drink?" I suggest.

He lifts an eyebrow at me, "Okay, yeah, sure."

We walk into the lobby together and go up the elevator, for some odd reason, I have this gut instinct that something is just off, not particularly with Nick, but just in general. It's probably just from the guilt I'm feeling or my nerves.

As we walk down the hallway, my gut instincts were right, he's leaned up against the wall, arms crossed, and one foot propped up behind him.

X is staring at us.

Fuck, fuck, fuck!

I don't have any idea what to do next. Nick notices my feet concreting to the floor beneath me. He looks down at me in confusion and then to him.

"Took you guys long enough," X says.

"Long time no see Nico," he snickers a laugh shaking his head.

"Wait, what?" I ask not really knowing which one of these guys I'm talking to.

"Uhh, hey X..." Nick says nervously.

"You two..know each other..?" I ask out.

X is the one to answer, "oh yeah, we go way back..don't we Nico?" he says shaking his head again.

"Millie, you should probably go," X suggests.

"No. I'm not going anywhere, I don't trust you right now." I say slightly scared.

"Yeah..you shouldn't," he says chuckling.

What the fuck.

"I'm gonna go, Em," nick whispers to me.

X chuckles, "You got a nickname for my girl?"

He starts to slowly take a few steps towards us with his hands in his pockets with eerie calmness. Nick is officially sweating bullets and so am I.

"I..uh..I didn't know she was your girl man." Nick says in a more confused manner.

Nick looks down to, "I'll call you later."

"No the fuck you won't," X says charging at Nick with lightning speed. Before I can even wrap my head around what's happening, X takes one single punch to Nick's face, knocking him out.

Nick has fallen to the ground and I have no idea what to do.

"What the fuck is wrong with you?!" I scream out to X.

"Me? Me? What the fuck is wrong with me?! You were just out with this fucking..." he kicks Nick in the side and spits on him.

"Would you fucking stop?! He's not even conscious right now!" I scold.

"Yeah like I give a fuck?" He says enraged.

I don't say anything.

He paces around, tugging at the roots of his hair, "Answer me this Millie, what does he have that I don't?" He asks frustrated.

"Trust X, what he has that you don't is that he has my trust," I say looking him in the eyes.

He stops pacing around and releases his hair taking a step towards me, to anyone else I'm sure they'd feel threatened, but I don't.

"You are fucking whacky in the head if you think you can trust this guy." He says pointing to the still unconscious man on the ground.

I furrow my eyebrows at him waiting for him to continue.

"He worked for me for two years Millie, I think I know a little better than you," he says chuckling with a laugh.

"He..worked for you?" I ask quietly.

Holy crap, when Nick told me he used to work with Penelope...it was at X's house...?

"I..uh.." I start saying and scratch the top of my head not knowing what to say.

"Yeah..he ain't no saint Millie, far the fuck from it," X says calming down only a touch.

"I'm not saying I am either because I sure as fuck am not but don't let him fool you into thinking otherwise." He says.

I nod my head slowly looking at Nick. How in the actual fucking world could this have even happened? Los Angeles is so populated how could it be that I just chose to work for a business where my coworker not only knows X but was heavily involved with his business? I understand people can change, I don't know the whole story but I'm pretty sure it doesn't matter at this anyway.

"I don't know what to do anymore Millie, I love you but you clearly can't make up your mind on what or who you want, I can't do this in between shit anymore," X says pacing around again.

"I told you I'd wait forever and I will if in the end, I know that you're trying to get there but I can't wait around if you're not taking it seriously, I don't want another woman in my life, I only want you but the feeling on your end are not reciprocated." He says stressed out.

"What do you want Millie?" He asks expectantly.

"I don't know X," I say honestly.

"Well figure it the fuck out and come find me when you do." He says shaking his head, turning his back to me, and leaving.

When X is no longer in view I look down at the unconscious Nick, "What am I supposed to do with you now?" I ask.

Chapter 56

POV

Millie

I sit along the wall in the hotel hallway with Nick still out. At first, I was afraid X may have killed him with that punch but I see that he's breathing. It's going to be really awkward if another hotel guest comes waltzing down the hall. Luckily, this floor is a pretty quiet one.

Nick starts to move a little, I think he may be getting out of his unconscious state. He opens his eyes and sees me looking down at him.

He perks up and scoots away from me like I'm the devil himself.

"Where is he?!" he asks frightened looking around.

Gee, guess I could count on him to protect me if I needed it...

"He's gone, Nick," I say.

"Why didn't you tell me you were X's?!" He asks belittling me.

"I'm not his, he doesn't own me," I say annoyed.

"Sorry.." he says trying to recover himself.

I lean my head against the wall behind me, "sorry about all of this." I say not looking at him.

"It's not your fault Millie, X is..." he says trailing off.

"I know, you don't need to explain, since when do you call me Millie?" I ask looking over to meet his eyes.

He shrugs his shoulders.

"You know we're both going to need explanations on this, right?" I say.

I give him my rollercoaster of a story and he tells me his.

Apparently, Nick, who is actually Nico, worked for X a couple of years ago to pay for college. He grew up on and off the streets and had an opportunity to live at X's house while getting his life in order. He admitted to having a rough history there but didn't go into details. He's trying to stray away from his old life, sort of like me.

Nick lets out a loud exhale, "Millie look, I really do like you but I can't keep seeing you." He delivers the message with such ease.

"Yup..kinda figured that was coming.." I say.

If it weren't him to do it, it'd be me.

"I'm sorry, I wish you the best," he says standing up and walking away the same path did not long ago.

"You too," I say inaudible, putting my hand out in a wave with his back to me.

I put my head in my hand, "why me?" I ask myself with an exhale.

I get myself up off the ground and unlock the door to my hotel room letting myself in. Steph isn't here yet, I really need to vent to her.

I walk over to the couch, lying down on it, and covering my face with my hands, I'm filled with stress from the last 35 days.

I don't know what to do about X, of course, I want him more than anything but can I trust him? Can he even trust me anymore? The door is open for me if I want him.

I think back to the episode of The Bachelor, 35 days ago every girl wanted X, I mean they still do of course but I'm the one, I'm the winner in all this. I've done my fair share of mess ups too and at the end of the day, he still wants me just as much as he did the day before. Tomorrow, and the next day, and the next I'll still be the one he chooses without the what-ifs.

But what if the winner of the show, or me in this scenario is the one questioning everything?

I lay uncovering my eyes and looking towards the ceiling contemplating my thoughts and feelings about X, about the future or no future at all. What if I give him another chance and what if I don't? Will I regret one or the other?

I stand up going to the bedroom, I pull open the bedside drawer taking the cocktail napkins X wrote out for me the other night.

Oh my god, I completely forgot the envelope of 20 answers! This week has been insanity for me it completely slipped my mind.

I turn the envelope over and slowly open it while sitting myself down on the bed next to me.

"Okay X, let's see what you want me to know."

Chapter 57

POV

Millie

I take the piece of white paper out of the envelope, the page is filled with black ink numbered 1-20 of things about himself. I take a deep breath in and deeper one out and start reading number one.

1. Until you, Julian was my only true friend
2. I didn't take the Colombia deal even though it was offered
3. I secretly wished my mom would've denied the $25,000 to stay in my life
4. I hate the business I'm in but it's all I've ever known
5. Sometimes I wish my mom would've taken me with her so I could've had a normal life
6. I hate that my mom had more kids
7. I have no desire to meet my siblings
8. I was afraid to get close to you because this business is brutal, love can be used as leverage.
9. The day you moved into the penthouse, was when I really knew I never wanted to see a day without you
10. I knew my dad was cheating on my mom for the longest time but never told her
11. The day my dad left everything to me was the day I lost myself
12. My first tattoo was of my own name at 16 on my arm done by Julian when he was 15
13. Yes, It was embarrassing and I regret it
14. I lay awake at night thinking about my overdose and how unfair that was to you
15. At age 15 I attempted suicide to escape this life but Julian's dad found me before I could try and talked me out of it, you are now the only living person besides me who knows that

16. Yes, I have killed someone, more than once.
17. The first time I killed someone, I was 17 and I went to my room and cried like a baby even though he wasn't a good person. I thought about how his family would never see him again because of me.
18. I feel like you are the only one that sees me
19. I really do love you
20. I want you to be happy even if it's not with me but I'm too selfish to tell you that in person

Tear after tear fall from my face, landing on the letter in my hands. My heart really breaks for him in some of these revelations. X was a man who was designed to be a certain way because of his upbringing and surroundings even though through that hard shell of his, is a good person. X is a person who was abandoned by his mother at ten years old and twenty-one years later he still yearns for that maternal figure in secret. This is not the life he wanted but it's the life he got. His mentality in life is to kill or be killed, the pressure he must feel to be a leader in his household must be tremendous. He's a man that lives in a lonely world and when I came around I pulled him out of that loneliness, only to place him right back there. X is not someone who can easily walk away and start over elsewhere like me or even Nick can, he's so tied to his roots. He may have more money than anyone would ever need but it's true, money cannot buy happiness. I gave X happiness and he returned the happiness to me when it felt so out of reach. We were both just getting by before we met each other, living each day without meaning, feeling empty, and simply just surviving. We found something special in each other that brought out the light in one another. This note means everything to me, him revealing personal secrets with me, confirms what a strong man he is.

I have a lot to think about, I have a much better understanding of X but just because I understand him doesn't mean we're right for each other. Will he fuck up again even if he doesn't intend to hurt me? At the end of the day, he is very tied to those roots, people can't change overnight.

Chapter 58

POV

    X

It's early in the evening, Friday. I haven't spoken to Millie since Wednesday after the harsh encounter we last had. Today is the day she gets to move into her apartment. Although I'm not necessarily happy about the other night, I'm happy for her. She gets the new beginning that she's been longing for. I think back to Wednesday night, seeing Millie with Nico, I didn't know my heart could break any further than it already had. They were going to the hotel room, what were they going to do? I can't even go there with that fucking thought, it kills me. When I left, she probably nursed Nico back to health and he probably used it to his advantage.

That night, I came home to a clean house, not a drop of evidence to be left behind from Adria. I laid in bed with the sound of that crack playing in my mind, I knew it'd haunt me. I've never killed anyone that way before but my options were limited that night. I couldn't have large amounts of blood in my house so I did it in a way that would keep it to a minimum. I thought about suffocating her, I may be an asshole but I'm not the devil, I wanted something quick. Even though Adria made me suffer mentally, I didn't have it in me to make her suffer physically for minutes on end.

Julian is here in the penthouse lounging on the couch with a drink in hand, I told him about what happened, everything that happened that night. He was indifferent about the whole Adria thing as I figured he would be and told me to keep giving Millie time to figure shit out in her head. If she wants to be with Nico I can't stop her, I meant what I wrote in those 20 answers, I want her to be happy even if it isn't with me. I would rather carry the weight of the pain while she takes a chance at happiness.

There's a light knock on the door and this time I know better than to think it'd be Millie. I open the door and it's Stephanie.

"Oh, hey, come on in, your lazy ass boyfriend is getting on my nerves," I say moving out of the way to let her in.

"You're not the only one," she rolls her eyes and laughs.

"Hey!" Julian says sitting up as we talk shit about him in front of his face.

"Oh, X, I have something for you," Stephanie says pulling out a white envelope from her purse.

"What is it?" I ask confused.

"It's from Millie," she says handing it over to me.

"Do you know what it's about?" I ask curiously.

"No, she didn't say, she just asked me to give it to you before I came here," she explains shrugging her shoulders.

The nervous look on her face either indicates that she really doesn't know what's in here or that she does but it's bad news.

"Uh, yeah, okay, thanks, I'm just gonna go open this in my room," I say scratching the back of my head nervously.

"Okay," she says quietly.

I turn away from her and go down the hall to my room. I'm nervous as fuck, I'm 99.9% sure it's a breakup letter. I almost don't even want to open it but I can't keep myself in delusion.

I sit on the corner of the bed with my feet planted on the ground.

I open the envelope, my fingers are trembling, it feels like there's something other than a letter in here.

I take out the letter from the envelope, there's a penny inside? I'm beyond confused, I hold the penny in my hand and unfold the letter with with my trembling fingers.

"Okay, here goes," I say to myself overtaken with anxiety.

X,

37 days, It has taken me 37 days to dislike you, to like you, to love you, to hate you, and to forgive you. No matter how hard I try, I can't

give you up, no matter how hard I try, I can't stop loving you, so the only thing I want to stop trying with you, is fighting myself for what I really want, fighting myself, you. Our lives may be nothing alike, but we are. We have an undeniable love and understanding for one another and without the other half of me, I'm not truly me. My mom always told me that in the rare occasion that when you throw a penny into a fountain, you should always give it to someone else when your wish comes true so that they can have the luck to have theirs come true. So, X, I give you my penny so that your wish too, can come true.

Love,

Millie

Oh, my fuck!

I was not expecting this in the fucking least. I have tears falling from my eyes but for the first time in my life, they're happy tears. I need to get to her, and I have a pretty darn good feeling I know where she is.

I rummage through my drawers looking for a penny. "Got it!" I say to myself as I pick it up the copper between my fingers.

I run out of the bedroom, Julian and Stephanie are sitting on the couch cuddled together, I've caught their attention with my frantic attempts to leave, and I throw Julian the penny.

"The fuck?" He asks in complete confusion.

I chuckle, "Go home guys."

I leave them in the penthouse as I fly down the stairs, the elevator is just not fast enough. I run through the halls until I reach the front door. I turn the knob and rush out the door.

There she is, sitting on the ledge of the fountain wearing my black hoodie. I can't help but smile like an idiot at the sight of her. I run down the steps, two at a time, and by some miracle, I don't fall. I run to the fountain out of breath and stand in front of her.

"Are you serious?" I ask her in disbelief still.

She nods her head and I drop to my knees in front of her, making my fists into a ball to the sky, "Thank you god, thank you!" I say to the heavens.

I stand up again, picking her up and twirling her around with a big sloppy kiss. She laughs at my childish behavior as I set her back down.

She cradles my face in her palms and shrugs her shoulders, "Xavier, what on earth is the point of being alive if you're not really living?"